HELLBOUND

HELLBOUND

TIM HAWKEN

dangerous™
little books

First Published in Great Britain 2010
This hardback edition Published 2012
by Dangerous Little Books www.dangerouslittlebooks.com

Cover Illustration by Christopher Page

ACKNOWLEDGEMENTS

FOR ME, this is probably one of the most important pages in the book and, most likely, will be one of the least read.

There are a great many people to thank for their help in the creation of *Hellbound*.

I would sincerely like to thank the following people for their invaluable contribution:

Michael Williams for his professional writing advice. CJ Werleman, author of *God Hates You. Hate Him Back*, for believing in the concept enough to convince his publishers to take a chance on it. Hobbsy, a wonderful teacher whose passion for literature is infectious and entertaining. Professor Brian Edwards, who assigned the creative writing task that kicked off the idea. Johnny, Nikki, Nat, Sam, Mum, Dad, Lincoln, Eli, Graylo and Tommy G for reading the draft material and providing honest feedback.

And finally to my wife Tara, who is at once my worst critic and my biggest fan. I love you like Michael loves Charlotte. This book is for you.

PART ONE
DAMNATION

ONE

HE PREFERRED TO BE CALLED ASMODEUS. This was all I knew about the man standing before me. In fact, I wasn't even sure if he *was* a man. When I looked directly at him, he appeared normal. But if I glanced out of the corner of my eye, I could see something else, something intangible. It was as if his true self was hiding in his shadow, which loomed dark and menacing on the wall, flickering in the firelight.

The fire shed no light itself but rather made the darkness more visible, creating doleful shades of grey throughout the room. The darkness seemed to suck all hope from me, making me restless and edgy, but this man, this 'Asmodeus', brought my sense of feeling back. His charismatic air held me totally in thrall. He talked with such passion and authenticity that even if he told a blatant lie, I would believe in its truth.

And what was he talking about? Himself. About how he got to be in his position and how his 'work' was always taken out of context.

"You look very confused when I say I'm just trying to help these lost souls make their way to Heaven," he said. "The reason you're confused is you think I'm speaking metaphorically. Well, my dear friend, take it very literally. You see, I may have introduced myself as Asmodeus, but let me run off a few of my more well known aliases. Now let's see: we have Mephistopheles, Beelzebub, Bafomet, Iblis, The Fallen One, Lucifer, The Morning Star, Lord of the Dark, The Devil, oh and my favorite, Satan."

My jaw dropped as I stared in disbelief at the madman in front of me.

"Now I've seen that look on many faces before," he continued. "That look of, 'oh my God, I'm stuck in a bad dream!' Well, this *is* happening. But please don't be put off by the negative connotations of my 'titles', if that's what you'd call them. This is real, Michael, this is very real."

A deep growl rumbled in Satan's throat and suddenly the fire exploded throughout the room. Satan spread his battered wings, skeletal and black, half draconian half angelic, his eyes turning into pits of oblivion, reflecting my horrified expression as I fell back onto the floor. He collapsed into his chair shaking with fits of laughter. The room once again fell into its despairing shade of grey.

"I'm sorry, Michael, I just couldn't help it," The Devil squeezed between giggles. "I love a good joke. I'm not all about wrath and destruction. I am on your side! Haven't you listened to a word I've been saying?"

My mind was reeling. I tried to think of how I came to be there, in that room. Nothing came. It was as if a veil had been draped over my thoughts, so that all I could do was concentrate on the moment at hand.

Satan clicked his fingers, chuckling. "A bit confused there, Michael? Don't worry, your memory will come back soon enough, although not all at once or it would be too much for you to handle. Remembering your own death can be pretty horrifying; remembering your life can be even worse!"

Dead? I was *dead*. I looked at my hands. They appeared solid. I rubbed my fingers over the palm of my opposite hand. I could hear the crackling of the fire clearly. *This isn't a dream, I know when I'm dreaming*, I thought. I looked around the room again. There was a light coat of dust covering the polished-wood floor, but no trace of footprints from where this man had been pacing back and forth in front of me. It wasn't normal. *He* wasn't normal. I looked at Satan closely and he smiled. He had a pointed chin, shiny-white teeth, high cheek bones, black eyes and two short horns protruding just above his thick, jet-black hair. *Am I really seeing this?* I thought. *Am I dead? Where am I? Am I in Hell?*

"You *are* in Hell!" The Devil confirmed with a smirk. "You're here because you are dead. But that's not the only reason you're with me. And, I might observe, you don't seem too surprised you're down here and not in Heaven."

The thing is, I wasn't surprised at Satan's remark. Even though I couldn't remember my lifetime, I somehow knew, or rather felt, that I deserved to suffer.

"Suffer? You will do no such thing down here. You'll do nothing but enjoy yourself!" Satan laughed.

It occurred to me that my thoughts were being read. This devil was in my mind!

"Oh please, Michael, you don't really think I could have made it to be ruler of the underworld without learning a few tricks along the way? Don't worry, my powers only extend to my realm. When I go up there," he said, pointing up with a clawed hand, "I lose most of my glorious power. That's why God always tries to get me to fight Him on earth; Armageddon, the final battle. He knows he has my measure."

A look of pure hate spread across The Devil's face. Disgust and frustration deformed him to the point where his eyes turned a deep yellow, as if filled with bile. His mouth dripped venomous spittle and his bared teeth twisted into points. I let out a muffled cry and, instantly, he returned to normal.

"Oh, sorry about that, Michael," he said cheerfully. "God and I have a bit of a past, but you'll learn the truth of that soon enough. Let me try to explain the essence of *why* you are actually here. Come with me."

Satan stood up, turned and walked towards the door at the far end of the room, motioning for me to follow. I quickly fell in step just behind him, as we walked out the door towards an elevator.

"An elevator?" I wondered aloud.

"Of course!" he said. "Do you think we'd live in caves down here while everyone else on the planet lives in houses and apartments? We are the future, Michael, not the past, and we have everything you need."

The elevator doors opened with a sharp sounding 'bing' and he ushered me inside. Satan reached up and pressed the button for floor 666.

"See," he said as he turned to me with a cheeky grin, "we even have a sense of humor in Hell!"

This *must* be a dream, I thought to myself. A vivid, horrible dream. I watched the elevator's shimmering silver doors close in front of me. Cheesy elevator music leaked out of a speaker in the roof, just as if I was riding any ordinary elevator in any ordinary building. The metal cage lurched upwards and The Devil started talking again.

"Hell, Michael," he said, putting his hand on my shoulder as if to reassure me, "isn't a place of suffering or torture, but a place of purgatory and rehabilitation. It's a bit like a jail really, but with a few exceptions." He paused and looked up at the floor counter as it rose slowly towards the number of the beast. "You see, people end up here because they have done something wrong and have not repented for their actions. They didn't care that what they were doing was wrong. In order that they 'purge' these 'demons' from their system they come to Hell, so they can be cleansed before entering Heaven."

I must have looked confused. I certainly felt that way. My head was swimming. Satan paused as if deep in thought before clearing his throat to continue.

"Let me use an example. Say a man loves to rape women. He does it for a portion of his life and then dies. His soul is befouled because of his crimes committed on the spirit of the women he defiled, and so he ends up here in Hell. He comes here because God does not want predatory rapists running rampant in Heaven destroying more souls. It's my job to help the rapist rid himself of his terrible urges. In other words, I rid him of his will to sin. I convert the damned to the saved. Once the rapist's soul has been cleansed then he can trot off to Saint Peter with the hope of passing through those pearly gates."

The elevator shuddered to a halt. Bing, the door opened into a room made completely of glass. I stood for a moment transfixed. We were overlooking a thriving metropolis, where constant movement whirled far below and lights shone from every building. We were at least twice as high as any other structure around us. I could see for miles in every direction. The city stretched beyond sight. Every road below branched out from the building we stood on. They were linked by twisted laneways and offshoots, to look like a massive spider-web. Red and black glowed throughout most of the tangled net of streets. Others were the darkest pitch. Below us, the streets were alive with movement. Tiny cars were zipping, weaving and dodging through the fast-paced traffic. It was organized chaos.

"This is my kingdom, Michael!" Satan said, sweeping his arm out in front of him. "Welcome to Hell."

TWO

MY MOUTH HUNG AGAPE as I looked out at the world of Hell. The Devil laughed and slapped me on the back like an old friend. He walked over to stand in front of the huge glass windows. I followed like a lost puppy.

Looking down below and around at the world outside, I barely registered what I saw. To the left a few miles away, a mountain jutted directly out from the otherwise flat surroundings. It was a twisted black crag of rock covered in gnarled, burnt trees which arched toward the boiling sky. A gigantic mansion perched on its peak, no roads going up or around the base.

"The only way up there is by chopper or dragon," Satan said. "It's my palace, Casa Diablo, atop of Mount Bilial. Let me give you a tip: it makes Hugh Hefner's Playboy Mansion look like a monastery!" He pointed to the far distance. "Straight ahead is the sulphur lake you've no doubt heard so much about in the classics. It's bordered to one side by a lake of fire and the other side is a lake of liquid ash. Together, they make the three eyes of Satan."

He sounded like a chirpy tour guide describing the pyramids of Egypt.

"We go fishing sometimes in the sulphur lake for giant crab-goblins. Very tasty eating."

He licked his lips with a forked tongue as I turned to look at the three lakes. They did indeed look like three eyes; one red, one black and the last, crystal blue. A thin smokey haze hung above them, blending the colors together to form a twisted kaleidoscopic cloud. I started to get a headache staring at the swirling colors in the sky. Blinking, I looked away and over to

6

the right to see beyond the city. Bare plains stretched out into the distance.

"That is the 'desert of the doomed'," Satan said solemnly, "where lost souls who have given up any hope of salvation go to roam aimlessly for all eternity." He quickly turned me away from the ghostly spectacle, sweeping his hand theatrically in front of us. "And here is the pride of Hell City. A den of diabolical debauchery, fetish and fun. A cross between Las Vegas, Amsterdam and Bangkok. The delicious suburb of Smoking Gun."

It looked as if it were straight out of a bizarre comic book. Themed casinos with flashing lights and neon signs made up the centre. They ranged from the grand to the grotesque. There was obviously no consideration taken about offending anyone, with one casino brashly named Cleopatra's Clitoris. It was a shining building in the shape of a naked Cleopatra, spreading her legs and pinching her left nipple.

"The nipple is the penthouse suite," Satan laughed.

Another building to the side of it, obviously a brothel, was called Magdalene's Mansion. There was a billboard posted on the side of the building advertising Bibles for sale! The list of stupefying establishments went on: glitz and glamor to be had at Castle Dracula, rare meats at Hannibal's Steakhouse and gay abandon in Liberace's Drinking Palace.

"It's like Disneyland for adults. Dead, sinning adults," The Devil said. "You can dine on all seven of the great sins, Lust, Greed, Gluttony, Pride, Sloth, Wrath and even Envy. There's gambling, sex, killing and torture. Everyone has fun in Smoking Gun. That's the suburb's credo."

"This isn't what I expected Hell to be like," I stammered, as I looked at the gaudy streets of Smoking Gun.

"What did you expect?" Satan asked raising a black eyebrow that framed an even blacker eye.

7

"Well," I replied, "Hell: suffering, unbearable heat, demons, the flames of damnation. A place where people come to pay for their sins."

"Ah ha!" Satan boomed. "Now we're back to it. The purpose of Hell! Most people, like you," he said, poking me playfully in the chest, "have it all twisted about. They think my job is to make people pay for their wrong-doing on Earth, to punish the evil for their sins. As I was saying before, Hell is more like a jail. Hell was designed by God to help the tainted souls of Earth become cleansed, so they can go on to Heaven. Unfortunately, just like a jail, some of the souls here become institutionalized and don't want to leave. Instead of *expelling* their demons, they *become* them. As for the heat," he said with a wry smile, "you're standing in an air conditioned building. It's a whole lot hotter once you walk outside."

I stepped back and looked at him, truly realizing for the first time this might not just be a nightmare. It was as if his talk of something as mundane as air-conditioning helped me connect everything he'd been saying with normal existence.

"Finally!" he laughed. "You're starting to accept this is actually happening. I must admit, it normally takes people a bit longer."

"So when you say that people become their sins, you mean that a human can turn into a demon?" I asked.

"They can and they do," he replied, nodding and smiling like it was the most normal thing in the world. "If a person is so insatiable that they will never have enough money or power, then they eventually turn into a Greed Demon, forever bound to Hell to tempt others into a life of voracity. Their skin slowly turns yellow and their eyes green. Ten fingers sprout from their heads, and their noses grow into a pig's snout. There are demons for every possible sin you can imagine. The idea is that other souls in Hell will see how deformed these demons have become in pursuit of their chosen pleasure, so they will no longer want to commit that particular sin."

"So, this isn't the end of the road then? There is hope?" I asked.

"There's hope for all," The Devil smiled, "but still there is not salvation for all. As I said, some cannot or will not be cleansed. Some become demons of their vice. While demons are meant to serve as a warning to those who would go down the same path, sometimes they can be very persuasive, and actually talk others into believing that murder or lust will give them the meaning they've been searching for. They recruit souls to become fellow demons of their sin, but I do my best stop that. You know, some of the demons aren't all that bad. Many even work for me. However, some are the purest evil and extremely powerful."

"So, some souls don't ever leave?" I asked.

A sneer ran across his draconian features. "Well, why would you want to leave here?" he snapped. "Aside from the smell of sulphur and the oppressive heat and darkness, this place is actually a lot of fun! You get to do whatever you want, however you want, to whomever you want, for as long as you want!"

"What's the catch then? Why would you leave at all?" I asked.

The Devil paused. His face clouded over momentarily, like he was recalling a traumatic memory. "Well, there are a few drawbacks," he admitted slowly. "One is that there is no law here, except jungle law. If you're weak, you are easy prey for the torturers, thieves and worse. We stop no-one from doing what they want to do, so Hell is governed by the powerful and the ruthless. People do suffer, but at the hands of others, not by my hand."

I was horrified. "So there is no punishment for the wicked after all. It's just like in life, where the mean spirited and selfish get what they want."

"Now wait a second," The Devil said. "I haven't finished just yet. There is serious punishment for those who think they can continue their evil ways without judgment. There is the guilt."

"Guilt?" I scoffed. "Demons and the damned don't feel guilt! All they feel is hate and anger. They don't care about what they do, as long as they get what they want."

The Devil started to really laugh. I was furious. This was no laughing matter. My belief in goodness was being shattered before my eyes, and he was laughing like a boy who'd just seen an enemy stub his toe.

Satan's laughter cut short. He looked me deep in the eyes with his flaming stare.

"You should know this," he said in an apocalyptic tone. "You should take heed, Michael. Never underestimate what I say. Never sell me short. You forget who you're talking to. I am Satan. The guilt that you will feel down here is like nothing you've ever felt before. It is the guilt of the condemned, the guilt of those deformed by desire and greed. You will feel it more acutely than you could ever imagine, and you will feel it thrust upon you six times each day. When the sky burns from horizon to horizon and black smoke swells out of the gutters." Satan's voice grew louder and louder as he spoke, fire dancing in his eyes as he ranted like a deranged priest in the pulpit. "When Hell's fire shatters the minds of every soul in Damnation, you will know where you are and why you are here. When the weight of every misdeed and sin is thrust down upon you like a crushing burden of menacing responsibility, you will know what you have done. You will feel the guilt. You will feel the haunting. It is enough to drive the most evil soul insane. It is unrelenting and it is absolute. Don't underestimate the power of a guilty mind. Never underestimate self-shame and self-destruction."

The Devil raised his clawed finger and pointed to the horizon. It began to flare and burst into a bloody vortex of flame, before blasting over the heavens of Hell. I collapsed as sharp agony shattered through my skull.

THREE

Sweat beaded lightly on my bare chest. I was only just getting started with this bum. Dancing around him on my toes, I sized him up. My muscles were full of energy, the thrill of the fight coursing through my veins. He looked tired already and we were only a minute in. He had a trickle of blood leaking out of the corner of his mouth, where I'd just clipped him with a quick left jab. A tight ring of jeering spectators stood around us, jostling to get a view of the action. They'd paid good money to watch us battle it out with bare fists.

The fight was in a dusty, disused warehouse on the outskirts of Las Vegas. The high roof absorbed the sounds of our shuffling feet. It was a blustery night outside, the wind rattling the tin walls of the structure with each howling gust. Large, fluorescent lights buzzed above us, sending harsh light through the interior. The warehouse was void of furniture except for a makeshift grandstand for the V.I.P.s in the center and a single table shoved in the far corner where the punters could place their bets. It was a lo-fi set up. It was also completely illegal, but that just added to the excitement. Plus the money was better.

My opponent moved in and popped me in the ribs with a lightning-fast right rip. I wheezed as the air went out of my lungs, but managed to jump back before he could capitalize on his hit. A roar went up from the crowd at the burst of action. Maybe he's not such a bum after all, I thought. We danced around a bit more, playing with each other. It's best to give these blood thirsty dogs their money's worth, that way I'd get paid better next time. Create a demand to see me. "He's hungry," they'd say, "a bit green, but he's got the look of the devil in his eye."

Stepping back to avoid a straight right, I surged in and unleashed four, quick jabs into his stomach. I leapt back out of range. Wear him down, make him hurt.

There were no rounds with this fight, no bells to be saved by. Just one long, punishing bout. I liked to pace myself when fighting like this. Tire the other guy out. "A tired opponent is a slow target," I kept telling myself as I circled him. We traded some light hits, nothing major. The crowd enjoyed it

11

though, egging us on. "Kill him! Get him!" A fat businessman drooled from the front row, clutching a bundle of betting stubs in his right hand.

My opponent moved in, feinting to his right to put me off. I saw it coming. Stepping to the side, I thundered a heavy left hook right into the high part of his cheekbone. I could feel the bones crack under the weight of my fist. Blood poured from his nose but he didn't go down, he just stumbled back into the crowd. They held him up and then pushed him back, lurching into the ring. "Get back in there," they yelled. "Finish him!" I heard someone cry from the side of me.

I watched as he rocked on his feet, eyes clouded with splattered blood from his nose. I took my chance, swinging hard and crushing my fist into his nose again. He dropped back, limp. The sound of flesh slapping on the concrete was drowned out by yells from the crowd, some of triumph and others of desperate loss. Hard earned money had been dropped on a dog that had 'only lasted five minutes'. In reality, that was a fairly long fight. I'd been in some that lasted seconds.

Trainers rushed in to pick their fighter off the floor. I raised my fist, but wasn't smiling. The excitement was over for me. I felt a stab of guilt from causing a fighter unnecessary pain by hitting him in an open wound. I could have just pushed the guy over and he would have been out for the count. Oh well, I thought, he'll recover. I've earned my money and he earned his.

I walked over to my corner where my coach slapped me on the back and threw a towel at me.

"Good work, son." I felt a surge of pride from making him happy. He was the only father I'd known.

I wiped myself down as Coach soaked my swollen hands in a bucket of icy water. I thought about the first time I'd ever met him. He had pulled me off the streets and taken me into his home when I was just sixteen. I'd been living in and out of shelters most of my young life. My parents had abandoned me at an orphanage run by the Catholic Church when I was just a baby. I'd lived there until I thought I was old enough to go out on my own. Coach had been passing by as I was brawling with another homeless teen in an alley over some food. He had just stood back and watched as I got beaten to the ground.

"You've got heart, kid," he had said, when he picked me out of the dirt and dusted me off, wiping the blood from my face. "You've got

12

skills too. You just need to learn not to pull back on the killing blow. When you show mercy you show weakness. Only the strong survive."

When he trained me, he'd yell it out in between sit-ups. "Only the strong survive. Pain is weakness leaving your body."

He made me continue my studies from the orphanage as well, constantly making me read books like The Art of War *and* The Alchemist. *"No use in having a strong body if you have a weak mind," he said. He was full of sayings.*

I sat down on a stool and started to unlace my boots, watching as the other fighter's trainer called out for a doctor. Something was wrong. I got to my feet and ran over.

"Hey," coach yelled from behind me, but I barely heard. By now a crowd had formed around the fighter's body, which still lay limp on the ground where I'd knocked him down. I squeezed through just in time to see the Doctor look up at me.

"He's dead," he said.-, "You'd better get out of here."

Dead? I thought, as my whole body went numb. I had killed him. It wasn't meant to happen like that. I was bundled out of the building and into a car. Dead bodies weren't a good thing at illegal boxing matches. Guilt overcame me. I started to cry. I felt sick. I needed air. Coach opened a window. I leaned my head outside, letting the icy night wind numb my face.

"Forget it, kid," Coach said from the back seat. "He knew what he was getting into. He knew the risks."

I wasn't listening. All I could think of were my opponent's blurring eyes, just before I had murdered him. I vomited down the side of the car as the wind buffeted my sagging head.

FOUR

I AWOKE ON THE GROUND in a huge glass room, at the feet of a smiling man dressed in black. It only took a moment for me to remember where I was.

"I hope that wasn't too painful." The Devil sighed as he helped me to my feet. "It's much easier for me to show you things rather than try to explain them."

"You mean that was real?" I asked. "That happened? That was really me?"

"It was." He frowned. "Unfortunately, that was just a small sample of what it feels like to experience the haunting of guilt you will receive in Hell. The first day you'll simply remember your life. You will have visions of the biggest turning points in your existence. Some of these will be your darkest sins. Some may be of your greatest redemptions, if you're lucky. After the first six visions you will know who you were in life, and therefore who you are right now. Every day after today, the visions will become the most hideous moments of culpability you could ever imagine. The Guilt: it's every terrible moment of your life visited upon you at once; every disappointed voice whispering in your ear; every victim of your sins eating at your soul. For some, it's completely unbearable. It's a horrible tool to use, but it is my most powerful in reforming the filth that inhabit this place."

"You don't sound like you enjoy having this kingdom of yours just as it is," I snapped, unsure how to react. I still felt the lingering sense of pain at what I'd just relived, but the feeling was fading quickly.

"Oh, come now," The Devil retorted. "Of course I enjoy it. This is my home, I rule here! If I sound bitter, it's because I didn't choose to live here. I was exiled to Hell by God against my will. I'm forced to do this, to cleanse these souls. If some didn't pass over to Heaven, then Hell would very quickly become choked with God's rotting souls of filth. Hell is not eternal like Heaven, we are finite. We cannot hold a constant migration of sinners to our shores. I cannot stand by or laze about, watching wave upon wave of souls come screaming into my home and do nothing. Then Hell *would* be eternal damnation for all!" Satan glossed over his outburst with a laugh. "At least it keeps me out of trouble. No rest for the wicked, ha ha!" He elbowed me in the ribs like it was the best joke in the world.

I became uneasy. I was in Hell and I was with The Devil. I'd just witnessed myself murder another man. It was my time for punishment. I accepted that it was deserved. I'd destroyed a life with my own hands.

"So," The Devil interrupted my thoughts again. "Is that really why you think you're here? For killing that other man who willingly stepped into a fight with you?" he laughed.

"Of course!" I spluttered. "Isn't that the greatest sin? Murder."

"Actually, it's not," he said and turned his back to me, walking away to the elevator where we'd entered the room.

"Wait a second!" I shouted, running after him. "I have murdered someone! Surely, this is why I'm in Hell. What is my punishment? Is that not why I am here?" I repeated.

Satan pushed the button for the elevator and turned to me.

"You have already punished yourself for that, Michael. It is a sin to kill, yes, but it's only a sin to kill without remorse, without a sense of responsibility. You are here to confront your sins, not suffer for them. Haven't you listened to me at all? All you need to do to get a ticket to Heaven is to face your sins, accept your responsibility for them, repent and promise never to do it again. But, if you so much as think about sinning again, you'll come plummeting back down to Hell with all the other lost souls, like a heroin addict relapsing into a cycle of fear and self loathing that could destroy your soul forever. Let's hope that doesn't happen to you though, eh?"

Bing! Satan's sentence was punctuated by the elevator doors opening. I stepped inside without even thinking. The doors closed as he moved in next to me.

"It's time to see the rest of Hell, Michael. It's time to confront your life. We're going to see all the nasty things you've done and hopefully some of your saving graces, if you had any. At the end of this, your first day in Hell, you'll be able to make the choice of whether you should be here or not."

"It can't be that simple," I said, more of a thought than anything.

"It is if you want it to be. However, it must be a choice with the utmost conviction. We don't like fence sitters here. There are no maybes at the end of the day, just I will or I will not."

FIVE

BING. The doors opened out into a huge foyer. Smokey grey floors extended up into walls. It looked like the building was made out of one massive piece of marble. There were no seams or cracks anywhere to be seen. Even the windows seemed to be made out of marble, wafer thin and clouded with white swirls, like souls trying to escape a mineral prison. There were no paintings or pictures on the walls and no carpet. The room was bare, sterile except for a reception desk near the main entrance. A beautiful woman sat on a stool behind the counter. She was wearing a silky, black dress, as if ready to go to a ball, or possibly a funeral. She had a headset on, raven hair pulled back tight and wrapped in a bun, with a curved knife stabbed through as the lynch pin. She looked up and smiled at Satan as we exited the elevator. Two rows of white, razor-point teeth framed with black gums. A phone rang on the desk and she answered.

"Hello, you've reached the office of The Prince of Darkness, how may I help you?" she said in an abnormally low-pitched voice, gravelly but still feminine. "I'm sorry, he's with an important client right now. Can I take a message?" She wrote a note on a pad in front of her as she nodded.

"This is Clytemnestra." Satan introduced me as she hung up the phone.

"Pleased to meet you, Michael," she smiled, exposing her murderous teeth again. "I've heard so much about you."

"I'm sorry?" I stammered.

Satan cleared his throat behind me and she shrank back behind her desk.

17

"Oh, you know, I mean, I read everyone's file that comes into Mr. Asmodeus' office. So I know who you are. No one can see Satan without my approval."

"I see," I said, somewhat irritated that this woman should know more about me than myself.

"Don't worry," The Devil chirped behind me. "That's what we're here for, Michael, to find out who you are. Let's take a ride and start your journey." He ushered me towards the front doors.

"Mr. Asmodeus!" Clytemnestra called after us as. "Joseph Stalin wants to know if you're still having brunch tomorrow."

The Devil opened the doors of the building, and we stepped out onto the streets of Hell.

SIX

THE HEAT HIT ME LIKE A SOLID WALL. It crushed me from all around and burned my throat with each breath, sending ripples of pain though my neck and into my lungs. My eyes watered and sweat began to weep from every pore in my body. I hadn't moved and I was already exhausted. I turned to face the street. Cars whizzed past at breakneck speed. Ferraris, Hummers and Monster Trucks, vehicles of every shape and size streamed past constantly. It seemed these souls didn't rest once they were dead. The grey-red light from the boiling sky above washed over the city. Concrete surrounded us. The buildings looked like they had grown from the soil beneath, rather than been constructed from the ground up. Graffiti covered some of the buildings; others were immaculately clean. There was no consistency. It added to my sense of disorientation. I would have collapsed if Satan hadn't have held my arm to steady me. He guided me off the curb and into an open limousine. The door shut behind me of its own volition.

I sat on black leather seats, letting the cool air-conditioning wash over me. I panted, covered in sweat.

"Warm, isn't it?" Satan laughed as he wriggled back into his seat. The tinted divider-window in front of us slid down, exposing a humanoid shark's ugly head. Its sharp teeth were caked in dried blood. The thing's lips moved but the teeth stayed firmly clenched together as it spoke.

"Where to, Sir?" it asked politely.

I noticed it was even wearing a chauffeur's cap and suit.

"The Sloth's Lounge," Satan said.

"Very good, Sir," the shark-demon said. The divider window rolled up as the car accelerated out into the chaos of Hell's traffic.

Black Sabbath played loudly through the stereo. *It's true what they say*, I thought to myself, *The Devil really does have the best tunes.*

"Damn right I do," Satan smiled at me.

The Devil sat with his eyes closed, humming to the music on the radio, tapping his knee as we lurched around a tight corner and down a busy road. Unsure what to do, I lapsed into silence. To be honest, I was frightened. I'd already seen myself kill a man today and I felt the most terrible regret. I knew that even though my victim put himself in that situation, I could've easily prevented his death by simply holding myself back from striking when I didn't need to. Now I was heading off with Satan himself to confront my other sins. The worst part was not knowing exactly what they were, or how I was to see them. I tried my hardest to push any thoughts from my mind as we raced through the streets of Hell, but the sense of foreboding ran thick through my skin, into my churning stomach.

I watched the city as it sped by. A concrete jungle wrapped up around me, high above to the bloody sky, which boiled with endless black storm clouds. Every few seconds, purple forks of lightening split the scene. We slowed to a halt at some traffic lights. A group of demons fought on the street corner. A giant, bug-like creature with an ant's head and scorpion tail was firing a gun into a pack of darting pygmies. The pygmies were throwing knives at him, in between dodging bullets. One of the knives caught the bug in the throat. He fell backwards howling as the pygmies swarmed over and tore him to pieces. A thought struck me.

"Can you die in Hell?" I asked, watching the carnage in front of us.

"No, you cannot," Satan answered. "You're already dead. However, the body you inhabit acts a lot like your body on earth. It's a casing for your soul, a vessel that needs to be maintained and looked after. It's very hard to separate body, mind and soul. They are the holy trinity of being. Separate any of the three and consciousness becomes incredibly hard to

20

maintain, for any meaningful period of time. Take our bug friend," he said, indicating the bloody mess on the pavement. "Because his body has been so severely damaged, he has lost the ability of conscious thought for now. However, unlike a body on earth, his parts will link and heal as one after some time. I like to think of it as an ethereal body; substantial enough to be pulled apart, but malleable enough to withstand total destruction. Unfortunately for him, those pygmies made off with his head. He'll now be suspended in a permanent state of unknowing until it is reunited with his body. So, I guess he is dead in a sense."

I considered what he'd just told me. Even if I was dead, I'd have to be careful not to fall in harm's way.

"Of course you'll have to be careful!" The Devil snapped. "You're in Hell, Michael; there are more predators down here than prey. Bear in mind you can fight back. Most demons are still so steeped in the idea of their earthly body that they can be knocked out the same as they could have during life. A sharp blow to the head, strangulation, goring; anything that would have caused unconsciousness on earth will do the same in Hell. Not for all though. Not for all," he added as an afterthought.

The traffic-light turned green and we sped forward again. The next block we came to, there were normal looking businessmen dressed in button-down shirts, milling in and out of buildings. Most were carrying briefcases, likely heading to their next meeting somewhere in Hell City. They looked like they were simply content to carry on with their lives like they were up on Earth, delving deeper into the greed and facelessness of multinational corporations. I thought of the thousands of millions of souls who now lived in Hell, all at varying stages of corruption, and all suffering the guilt of their sins. I wondered if my parents were out there somewhere. I could be driving past them right now and not even know. I'd never even laid eyes on a picture of my mother or father.

I could see we were getting closer to the suburb of Smoking Gun. The lights slowly grew brighter and less red. Greens, yellows and blues lit up the skyline, the whole world taking on a neon glow. Whores walked the streets, dressed to impress in lace-topped stockings and high-heels, many wearing nothing at all. Some pulled 'tricks' off the main drag into the nearby brothels or dark alley-ways, to ply their carnal trade.

Drunken gamblers stumbled from building to building aimlessly, like mindless drones getting drawn in to the succubus casinos, whose games slowly squeezed their souls of all innocence, driving them closer to being true demons. The whole place made me feel sick to the stomach. It didn't seem like this was a place of reformation.

The car slowed and pulled up to the curb in front of a large building with an unkempt sign over the entrance that read, 'Sloth's Lounge'. Satan stopped humming and his eyes snapped open.

"Oh good, we're here!" he said happily, opening the door and letting the heat bubble into the car. It was like a vice clamping around my body. "Just push through it," Satan said as he calmly slid out of the limo and pulled me out onto the street.

Everyone around us stopped. A few of the demons closest to us bowed down onto the pavement, groveling at our feet. One was covered in black scales, and another had sagging, pink skin, bald all over, like a Sphynx cat. They wailed in satanic prayer as The Devil looked on unimpressed. One seemingly normal person turned and ran off screaming, while others simply stared and whispered.

The Devil buttoned up his jacket and laughed. "This is what it's like to be famous, Michael, some people love you, some are scared of you and the rest are just plain jealous."

Satan took me by the arm and we walked through some extremely grimy doors into a smoke filled room. I looked through the haze to see beanbags strewn all over the ground, bodies laying askew everywhere. Televisions were bolted to every possible piece of space except for the floor. Even the roof was covered in flickering screens. Zombie-like creatures slept all around us. The ones that were awake stared at the screen closest to them, some eating food and others drinking strange concoctions of god-knows-what. They were slurping and spilling the liquid over the carpet and themselves with each sip.

No one so much as looked at us, like they couldn't be bothered wasting the energy. I peered closely at one person as we walked past and saw that his skin was in fact, peeling off his face. It was as if he was decaying as he lay there, eyes closed, breathing softly. A slightly more animated pair of souls sat against a wall playing a computer game. The words 'World of War Craft Corner' flashed brightly on a sign above them.

Satan picked his way through the minefield of rotting, barely-moving corpses, over to the bar where he took a seat. A large creature covered in long black hair, with three curved spikes for fingers, very slowly made his way over to us. After a painfully long time he got to where we were and said in a drawn out whisper, "Hellooo Mr. Asssssmodeus, howwww are you? To wwwhat do I owwwwwe the fine plllllleasure of having you in my loouuuunge?"

"Sloth, this is Michael," he said in answer, then turned to me and added, "Sloth is the creator of this maze of malaise, this lounge of laziness. This is where souls who are too languid or too scared to do anything come to literally rot their existence away. They melt into beanbags and couches while they watch TV, play video games or just do absolutely nothing. Some of them don't even bother to breathe anymore, since they don't need to because they're dead. " He smiled. "This is a place of inactive sin, the sin of not making the most of your existence. For my money it isn't as bad as killing or raping, but, according to God, a sin nonetheless. It's actually kind of ironic that the only true sloth in here is the busiest. Hey, Sloth?"

"What'ssssss that?" The creature behind the counter asked, as if waking from sleep.

"Oh nothing," The Devil smirked at me. "Fetch us two bottles of Heineken, Sloth, on the double," he shouted, clapping his hands in command.

Sloth turned ever so slowly and shuffled towards the back of the bar to a fully stocked fridge.

"He'll be at least half an hour," Satan joked. "Everything around here takes a long time, since these souls have an eternity to do it."

I looked around the room a little more. *How could people do this to themselves?* I thought, as one indolent soul finished a huge plate of nachos and then flopped back down on his back. I could smell the corroding flesh, wafting over to me from the floor, where the bulk of zombies lay. I scanned each television in the lounge for something interesting. Some programs I recognized, like *Baywatch*, but strangely the biggest television screen looked like it was showing the evening news.

"What's that show over there?" I asked Satan, pointing to the huge flat-screen on the closest wall. "It looks like most TVs in here are playing pretty much the same thing."

"Oh that?" Satan yawned, as if he was taken up in the spirit of the lounge. "That's Earth."

Unsure I had heard correctly, I pressed him. "You mean The Earth? You watch what we do on Earth?"

The Devil sat up in his chair, suddenly more alert. "It's only one of Hell's favorite past times!" he said, pointing up at one of the closest screens. "Look at how entertaining it all is! Just think about how well your pathetic attempts at 'reality TV' rate on Earth. We have the ultimate reality show running non-stop with no breaks for all of eternity. Every day we get new characters, multiple love plots, steamy affairs, hilarious games, and delicious murders. Not to mention when a war is on, which mind you seems to be all the time. Humanity is never more volatile than during wartime. Such a paradox: everyone so compassionate and loving to all in their own country, but all of that balanced out by the intolerance and hatred they feel for 'the enemy', who most of the time are almost exactly the same as them. The only difference between opposing sides is the fact that they worship a slightly different idea of God, or live on a piece of land the other side want or say belongs to them. The most hilarious thing of all: the majority of people on earth outwardly hate and oppose war, yet seem to be forever participating in it one way or another anyway, because of the manipulation of an elite few! I could go on for hours. This is one great show, Michael, the spectacle of Man!"

I couldn't believe it. Yet there it was right in front of me. Now that I looked closer, it seemed like each television was following a certain person, or covering a specific event. They were subtitled underneath, explaining who each person was, and what they were thinking. I stopped watching, afraid I'd spark off another painful memory by seeing a person or a place that I'd known during my 'life'.

"Oh, don't worry about that," Satan said, looking at me.

I jumped at his words, still getting used to him reading my thoughts.

"The memories will come to you like clockwork," he said looking at his watch. "In fact, you're just about due for another one."

A low moan started to come from all of the bodies around us, growing slowly louder and louder until all in the room were sitting up, screeching and holding their ears, rocking back and forth. The noise grew to a fever-pitch. I looked at Satan, afraid.

"What are they doing?" I asked.

"It's the guilt," Satan frowned. "They can feel it coming."

25

SEVEN

I sat unmoving on a stool in front of the twinkling machine, my hand perched on the 20-lines button. Every couple of seconds, I put a small amount of pressure on my finger so the machine could suck some more of my money away. If I was lucky enough, the right row of icons would line up and I'd get a flurry of noise and light to remind me that I was alive. I wished I wasn't.

Looking slowly around at The Riviera Casino, I wondered how many of these other people were like me; whiling away the hours with as little stimulation as possible, not wanting to sleep or to go home to a pitiful existence. The walls oozed forty years of cigar smoke, stale and rank no matter how much air-freshener they sprayed in the place. Like me, the building was a shadow of its former self. A few fresh coats of paint couldn't hide the fact that The Riviera was well past its prime. The bling had walked out and moved to the other end of The Strip. I don't know why, but it gave me odd comfort being somewhere that was slowly sliding into ruin. I felt at home.

Since that fateful fight, I'd crawled back up into myself. I had walked out on Coach, who refused to believe I didn't want to fight for a living any longer. "It's all you know," he'd say to me. "It's what you were born to do, you're a survivor. Don't run away from your talents." But that's exactly what I did. Even though I knew the people I fought signed up for it, even craved it like I had, I didn't want to destroy another life.

I delivered a rare smile. Three pyramids meant I'd just received the special feature. I could now sit back and do nothing while the wheels turned in front of me and rolled out my fate. Little victories took away the pain for a short while. It wasn't for the money, like most people think. The slots for me were for the feeling you get when everything falls into place at the right time to reveal a result you want. Only a minor win this time. I was almost out of coins.

The electronic spinning-wheel finally drained away the last of my money for the week, that is until my next welfare check kicked in. I looked at my watch: 2am. I'd been there for sixteen hours straight, no wonder I was so hungry. I picked up my warm, flat beer and staggered toward the exit, stiff

26

from sitting down for so long. My body felt like a dead weight. A fat, white gut wobbled beneath my clothes. My fighter's body had been drained into a beer bottle. I sucked down the rest of my bitter drink and tossed the plastic cup in the bin. Alcohol just didn't seem to affect me anymore. It used to mercifully dull my mind. Now it was just another habit.

I walked into the freezing night and breathed in a mixture of car fumes and plastic culture. A crisp breeze chilled my face as I ambled, slowly up The Strip towards The Stratosphere. I looked around at the neon lights of the city, not really wanting to go home. It was a fake mess of concrete and polish all around me, towering above my worthlessness. I sighed. So my life had come to this nothingness, anonymity in a city of nobodies.

I pushed past the seedy pimps clicking strippers' business cards at me and trudged towards my car. It was parked in a dirty car-park shoved between two beaten up all-you-can-eat buffets. They both had signs in the front saying 'voted best buffet on The Strip'. It seemed everything in town had been voted the 'Best in Vegas' at some time or other. They all clung on to those accolades like they were Nobel Prizes. I almost tripped over a pair of legs protruding from a doorway to my right. Regaining my balance, I swore under my breath at a man who sat shivering beneath yesterday's newspaper. He looked up at me with dirty blue eyes from his hollow in the wall. He had a large, hooked nose that curved down, almost touching his top lip, and high-arching eyebrows, which made him look surprised, even though he was just looking at me with a blank expression. A tattered, grey wool beanie sat precariously on his head, like it could fall off at any moment.

"Could you please spare some change for an unfortunate stranger, kind sir?" he asked politely.

My frustration at the bum melted into a hot mixture of shame and pity. I'd been on the streets before. I knew how cold the winter nights of Las Vegas could be, chilling your bones to the marrow. When people think of Vegas they think of heat and lights, but the neon did nothing to cut though the bitter, close-to-freezing temperature in the dead of a January night.

"I'm sorry, friend," I replied humbly. "Those damn slots took the last of my change."

"I take VISA," he said, breaking into a warm, gapped-tooth grin. "Just swipe your card in my machine here." He held up an old plastic tape player next to him.

It was heart breaking. He was obviously a couple of forks short of a fondue set. I looked at his side where a half-torn teddy bear lay, placed purposefully upright and out of the dirt. My heart went out to this poor soul, down and out on his luck.

"I tell you what," I said to him. "I've got a comfortable couch you can sleep on for the night and some cans of soup we can eat for dinner, if you'd be nice enough to join me."

He actually shrank back into the doorway, as if he was afraid of my invitation.

"Why would you do that?" he asked, his voice full of suspicion.

"Because I have nothing else to offer," I said simply. "You can take it up or not, but I'm no wolf, you can trust my hospitality. It's better than a cold, tiled doorway for the night, isn't it?"

I didn't quite know why I was trying to talk him into it. I felt I owed him for some reason, not having had any money to offer when I should be able to toss him a couple of stray coins.

"Well, I guess I have nothing to lose really, do I?" He smiled again, picking himself and his teddy bear up. "Where are we going?"

I opened my sorry excuse for a car and jumped in the driver's seat as the beggar crept into the passenger side.

"I'm not far. In North Vegas," I said. "I have to warn you, it's not too fancy, but at least it's warm."

"Much better than the frigid pavement," he said trying to lighten the mood. "My name is Dante, kind sir, and you are?"

"Michael," I said, holding out my hand.

He shook it with firm vigor.

"Pleased to make your kindest acquaintance, Saint Michael," he smiled. "Thank you for showing some mercy on a wretched creature whom deserves none of it."

"Oh come now!" I laughed as I pulled my car out onto the street and revved toward home. "Everyone deserves a bit of kindness every now and then, no matter what they think of themselves."

He frowned sadly and looked out of the car window as a light rain began tapping on the glass, breaking up the low hum of the engine. I sat silently for a little while, not sure what to say to this stranger sitting next to me.

"Did you ever used to be someone?" he asked after a few moments.

"Excuse me?" I replied, unsure what he meant.

"I used to be someone," he continued. "I used to be a successful family man. I used to be a father, a husband, an artist. I used to be someone," he said, more to the lights outside than to me. I stayed silent, keeping my eyes on the road.

"I lost it all, though," Dante continued. "I worked too hard, I didn't sleep, or rest or pay attention to the outside world until it was too late. They tell me I lost my mind, but I don't feel any different. My wife and daughter had to leave me because they couldn't understand me. My wife said she couldn't recognize me anymore, but I don't look any different than before. They took me away, the men in white. All I've got of my old life is my daughter's bear, Virgil. He's the only friend I have now, isn't that right, Virgil?" he said to the bear in his lap, tapping it playfully on the nose.

I wondered if you could actually be crazy if you knew you'd gone insane. Could you really have lost your mind if you were aware that it had happened?

"I've never been anyone," I answered. "I was born as nothing, with no-one and that's how I plan to die."

He looked at me with his melancholic, blue eyes. "Well that's just horrible," he said. "Surely there's more to it than that, more to you. What about family?"

I shook my head, keeping my eyes on the road rather than looking at him with my shame-filled heart.

"No friends? No lovers?" he asked.

"None I care to think about," I answered shortly.

"But we are nothing without love!" he gasped. "We cannot function without the driving gift that God has given all humans."

"There is no God." I said in reply. "There is only the devil. He is the only one I've seen proof of in my life."

"How can you say that?" he exclaimed, almost jumping out of his seat. He wound down the window furiously and stuck his hand out in the wind. He pulled it back inside the car, white from cold and dripping with raindrops. "Where do you think this miracle comes from? Water, which falls from the sky that feeds the land? In the desert no less! Now don't give me that nonsense about condensed evaporation forming clouds. This is from Heaven and nowhere else." He licked his hand. "Mmmmm, it's sweet."

I remained silent, unwilling to argue with Dante. There's no reasoning with the unreasonable, I thought. I steered the car into the gravel driveway *of my apartment block, a square edifice of brick veneer that jutted out from unkempt gardens. I got out from the car and Dante followed, hugging Virgil to his chest. I rattled my keys to find the right one, feeding it into the lock. It turned and I swung the door inwards. I flicked on the light to illuminate the interior of my ramshackle apartment.*

"By god, you've been robbed!" Dante yelled, looking at my squalid existence. I had no T.V., no stereo, no items of any monetary value, just books strewn all over the floor, amid dirty clothes and old newspapers. A sorry excuse for a couch was wedged in the corner.

"It's okay, Dante," I said, calming him down. "I told you it wasn't much, but this is home."

"Ohhhh, well it's just beautiful," he said cheerily, as if he'd forgotten his initial reaction. "It's a palace, a wonderful Mahal; I love what you've done with the place."

"It's okay, Dante," I said again softly, "I know it's a dump. Now, how about that soup? I don't know about you but I'm famished."

I walked to the cupboard and pulled out two tins of my favorite, minestrone, turning on the rusty electric stove. I slopped both tins into a pot and placed them on the cooker, then turned back to Dante, who now sat quietly in the corner reading one of my books, absent-mindedly stroking his teddy bear. I watched him as he read, flicking the pages backwards instead of forwards. He looked back up at me watching him.

"You must have been someone," he said to me, resuming the conversation from in the car like it had only just happened.

"Why's that?" I asked him. "Anyone can be no-one if they've done nothing."

"But what about this picture?" he said, holding up a Polaroid he had taken from the pages of the book in his lap. It showed me after one of my early fights, Coach holding my arm in the air in victory. I turned my back on Dante and pretended to check on the soup. I thought I'd thrown all my photos away, but I must have left that one as a bookmark and never taken it out.

"That was from another life," I said, burying my head in the fridge to avoid looking at him. "Do you want a drink?" I yelled from inside the refrigerator, as the cool air swirled around my embarrassed, burning face. I held a six-pack of beer above the fridge door to get his attention.

"So you were someone, then!" he said in answer, "and yes please, I'll have two cans if that's quite alright with my host, I'm very thirsty."

I took an extra six-pack from the fridge, laughing at Dante despite my shame at him finding my photo. Dumping the cans on the bench, I then poured hot soup into two bowls and took them over to where the bum was sitting on the floor, reading the book again. I looked at the pages. It was Midnight's Children *by Salman Rushdie. It had been one of Coach's favorites.*

"Here you are," I said to Dante, passing him his two beers and bowl of minestrone.

"Thank you kindly," he said, placing the book lightly to the side. "So why do you say that photo was from another life? Did you lose your marbles as well? Did the stress get to you like it did to me? Do you ever want to fight again? You still look young, if a bit out of shape -- too many of these ones," he said shaking his can of beer innocently.

I sat back, defeated. There was no getting angry at Dante. He was like a child, not really knowing what he was saying. Before I could stop myself, I said it.

"I killed a man, and now I'm afraid." I quickly pressed the cold aluminum of the beer can to my mouth and drained its contents, scared I'd never stop talking if I didn't plug myself with alcohol.

"I see," Dante answered happily. "Well, there's no dishonor in being afraid. I assume it was an accident, killing the man? I mean, you haven't murdered me yet, so it's obviously not in your heart to just go around ending lives, now is it?"

"Of course not!" I snapped.

"So why let your fears rule you? That's where the shame lies, not in an accidental death. The real disgrace is in killing yourself slowly with gambling and beer."

I stood up, now angry as hell at this stranger in my house. "And what would you know?" I roared, sending soup flying onto the carpet. "You're no better than me, living on the streets and begging for money. Your only friend is a crappy, filthy, children's toy with stuffing hanging out of it!"

Dante looked down at Virgil with tears in his eyes. He picked him up, stroking his head. "He didn't mean that, Mr. Virgil," he said. "You're a beautiful bear. Come on let's leave him alone, he's angry at us for telling him the truth; some people don't like hearing what they already know. Let's let him sleep." He got up and started to walk out the door.

"Please wait!" I called after him. "I'm sorry, I didn't mean it."

Dante turned slowly with a sad face. He pressed the bear's mouth to his ear.

"Virgil says he knows you didn't mean it, he wants to stay, Mr. Michael, if that's alright, it's too cold for him out there."

"Of course," I said, my anger melting away. "I'll get you some blankets, you must be tired."

I hurried to the cupboard before he could change his mind and pulled out my only spare blanket. I made the couch into a bed for Dante while he watched me quietly. I'd obviously scared him with my outburst. Once I'd finished, I turned to him.

"I'm sorry I yelled at you. Please, sleep and stay here as long as you want to. I'll let you sleep. I'll just be in the other room if you need anything."

Afraid to say anymore, I walked into the other room and flopped down on my bed. I felt so ashamed that I'd snapped at Dante. He was right. I was afraid, and I was killing myself passively. My life had turned from constant activity to a life of forced laziness. My world consisted of drinking beer, reading books and playing the slot machines at a casino. The only reason I went there, instead of the bars was because the Riviera never closed and no one seemed to notice if you stayed there all day every day. My life was slowly accumulating to a large heap of nothing.

I lay on my back and stared at the ceiling, trying to stay awake. As much as I loathed being awake, I hated sleep even more. My dreams showed me what I could have been. What I never was. They haunted me with visions of a mother I never knew. Many nights I also dreamt of dying in violent and horrible ways. I could never make myself wake from those dreams. My eyelids grew heavier and heavier. As hard as I tried to stop them, they crept down over my eyes. For the first time in over a week, I slept.

I awoke with the smell of my mother's perfume still in my nostrils, like jasmine flowers. As usual, I never saw the detail in her face, just a black outline, her smell and a sense of despair. It felt like I'd only just fallen asleep, but the grey light coming through my window told me it had been at least a few hours.

I heard the front door close softly and I jerked alert in my bed. I recalled the events of the previous night. I had brought a mentally unhinged stranger into my house -- Dante. I jumped up and ran into the lounge. The place was its usual mess, but there was nothing missing that I could see. The couch had been slept on, but there was no sign of Dante. I opened the front door and looked down the driveway. There was no one around. The ground was still moist from the sprinkle of rain the night before. I could see fresh, bubbling footprints in the gravel leading away from my unit and down the street. Dante had obviously just left. I almost ran down the road after him to make sure he was okay. I'd actually enjoyed the company of another person in my home, even if he was slightly crazy. I was alone again. I needed a beer.

Opening the fridge I reached in, but the normal stack of cans was gone. In their place was a note, the photo Dante had found the night before and a skipping rope. Taking the bundle out of the fridge, I put the contents on the kitchen bench. The note was scrawled in a beautiful, open cursive script. It read:

> Dear Saint Michael,
>
> I thank you for your kind gesture and hospitality in letting us sleep in your home. Virgil hasn't slept so well in all the time I have known him. We are truly grateful.
>
> I found this skipping rope buried in the back of your cupboard when I was searching for a pillow. I think that you should use it to become a somebody once more.
>
> Don't let the past rule your future, Michael, you still have your mind. I suggest you use it and begin your journey into a life of consequence, rather than letting it slip away like mine. A man much better than I once said that "a life lived in fear is a life half lived." Listen to those words.
>
> Mr. Virgil insisted that we take your alcohol also. I'm sorry, but there was no convincing him otherwise. He says it makes you fat and lazy, and that we would be doing you a favor.
>
> Goodbye, Michael, from both of us and good luck whatever you decide to do.
>
> Sincerely,
> Dante A.

I put down the note and looked at the photo of me smiling with my arm in the air. Those were some of the only days in my life that I was actually happy, where I felt like I was worth my skin. I picked up the skipping rope. Maybe it was time I started living again.

EIGHT

MY EYES FLUTTERED OPEN to see Satan smiling at me, holding out a beer.

"Here you are, Michael. Sloth finally got back to us with those drinks."

I pushed the bottle away as I sat upright again on my stool. It took a moment to readjust to my surroundings. I looked around Sloth's Lounge to see the bodies of the most languid souls in Hell, lying scattered around me on the floor, rotting and withering away. They were content watching others' lives on television, rather than living their own existence. I thought about the part of my life I'd just relived. It was a time where I was also wasting my life away like these souls. It made me feel ill. How could I wallow in self-pity like that? How could I run and hide away from myself, drowning myself in alcohol and smothering my senses with the false hope of slot machines? I hated who I was. I began to despise God for the lack of opportunities I'd been given. Born parentless, then out on the streets. I picked myself up, only to be knocked down by a twist of fate: killing a man during an arranged fight. What hope did I have?

"Oh, come on now, Michael!" Satan said, moving his face into my line of sight. "You can't just blame God for all of your downfalls; that will simply prolong your stay in Hell. Now, I'm not defending him," Satan laughed, "but we have to take responsibility for ourselves, even if we have been given a raw deal! Look at me, for example. I've been shafted more than anyone in the history of the universe and damn right, I'm furious, but I don't go around whining all day about it. I get on with my lot and am thankful for the purpose it gives me. I also take joy in the fact I'm going to have my revenge one day!" His eyes lit up with a brief flicker of insane malice before he looked away.

"But this isn't about me," he grinned, turning back to face me. "Think about what you just saw. You were down and out, but don't forget the saving graces. You showed kindness to a stranger and a commitment to get back to living. This is exactly the purpose of the visions, to show you not only why you could wallow in Damnation for eternity, but how you could easily make the choice to cross over to Heaven. You see your sins with new eyes and can better your decisions when the time comes. It's easy to judge others, Michael, but much harder to judge yourself. Most people rationalize their sins, their destructive actions. By seeing yourself again, afresh, you can cut away the pretense, the bullshit excuses and strip yourself bare. You can see yourself for who you really are. But we're not finished yet. We've got more layers to peel back, more of your life to see. Cheers!" He tipped his beer in my direction and then lifted the bottle to his mouth, taking a deep drink.

"Ahhhhh, I love it," he sighed, looking at his beer and then back to me. "The most important thing of all, Michael, is to learn to enjoy life and accept things for what they are. Take this beer for example. It's a tasty drink and nothing more. It's not a crutch or a vice if you don't want it to be. Now have a drink with me and stop being such a downer!"

The Devil pressed the green bottle of amber fluid in my hand and chinked his own bottle against it, taking another sip and looking me directly in the eyes, as if challenging me to take a swig. I took his cue and sculled deeply. God knows I needed a drink after what I'd been through in the last few hours. The beer slid with ease down my throat, the light bubbles tingling my tongue. It was cold and refreshing. I savored the taste, swirling the drink around in my mouth before gulping it down. I slammed the bottle on the bar and got up out of my chair.

"Alright then, Satan," I said, with new determination. "Where do we go next? What do we see now?"

"There you go, Michael!" he laughed, jumping up. "That wasn't so hard -- and look, you haven't turned into a lazy sod after all. Let's move on out of this dump, it's time to go to The Pit."

Satan waved goodbye to Sloth behind the bar as we picked our way through the garbage-heap of lost souls, who slept on the stale ale carpet. He pushed the doors open and the heat of Hell engulfed us. This time I was ready for it. I braced myself and pushed through, with the resolve to move through this Day of Judgment as quickly as possible. I had already seen part of the train wreck that was my life. I was still apprehensive about seeing the rest but accepted there was nothing I could do to stop it from happening. I had already lived it.

The masses racing along the street stopped dead on cue and we walked into their midst. They whispered and pointed, offering prayers as we passed by, many dropping to their knees. Satan barely seemed to notice. He ushered me back inside the white limousine we'd arrived in. The leather of the seats squeaked as I shuffled over to make room for The Devil behind me. The cool air of the interior gave me a reprieve from the blistering temperature outside. Satan shut the door and rapped heavily on the divider window, yelling, "To The Pit, Driver, with haste."

We screamed off the curb and I was thrown back into my seat. We wove in and out between cars, accelerating the whole time, going faster and faster. We must have been going over two hundred miles an hour. I gripped the door handle and sat back, fumbling for a seatbelt.

"Oh don't worry about that," The Devil grinned at me, "you're with The Dark Lord, I won't let us crash!" He waved his hand and all the cars on the road parted like a zipper before us. We surged forward even faster, the City of Hell whipping by in a blur. I tried to calm myself, breathing deeply, looking straight ahead, telling myself I couldn't die, since I was already dead. The Devil let out another laugh at my side. He was enjoying making me squirm.

36

"You're damn right I am," he quipped, pulling his usual mind reading trick. "We can't let you get too comfortable down here. You might never leave." He slapped his leg and laughed again.

"So, where are we going now?" I asked, forcing a smile.

"I told you, we're going to The Pit," he said as if that explained everything. "Don't worry you'll like it. It's an entertainment venue."

"What kind of entertainment?" I asked suspiciously.

"A bit of this and that; live music, avant-garde theatre, tawdry burlesque shows, you know, the norm. There's probably not too much you'll see here that you didn't see up there." He smiled, pointing to the ceiling. "Well actually," he giggled, "there may be a few things."

NINE

THE LIMOUSINE SLOWED TO A HALT at a ticket gate. A swinging billboard hung above us. It read in blood-script letters, 'The Pit'. I looked out the window and caught a glimpse of the toll collector talking to our shark-faced driver. It had a large, bulbous, octopus body with suction cups running the length of eight tentacle-like arms, which still had masculine, human hands on the ends. He waved them around and made gestures while his beak opened and closed, making clicking noises. His whole body shimmered from a light pink then deepened to a storm-cloud purple and back again as he spoke. Finally, he sat back in his chair and pulled a lever at his side. The boom-gate opened and we rolled through as the Octodemon strained to look inside our car. Satan sat staring straight ahead, his hands crossed in his lap.

We snaked through a gigantic car park, past every kind of vehicle imaginable. I even saw a couple of hovercrafts. Finally, our car slowed to a halt in front of a deserted section of large razor-wire fence, which spread around as far as I could see. I looked through, but could only make out a faint-green glow coming from the ground near a hand rail, which sat about fifty feet inside the fence. A faint thumping sound beat in the air. Satan opened his door and stepped outside. I followed without much thought. We were obviously here for a good reason. Satan knocked on the driver's window. It rolled down to expose our predatory chauffeur.

"Wait for us here," Satan instructed. "We won't be more than a couple of hours." He turned back to me. "Sometimes, people stay here for days," he explained, "including myself, depending on the entertainment of course. Follow me, we'll check out the view before we take our seats."

Satan turned and walked toward the fence holding out his hands out in front of him. As soon as he touched the links in the fence they melted away in a hiss of dissolving metal. He stepped through, quickly pulling me behind him. As soon as we were through, the fence hissed again. I looked back to see the alloy chain-links growing back together like they were alive. It would take a long time for me to get used to Hell, I thought.

"You'll never get used to it," Satan said flatly. "It's always changing, so as soon as something seems normal it gets twisted about. I can't let people settle into a routine, since routine provides comfort. It's just another reason to make souls want to leave. Most people hate change; personally I embrace it."

I was about to reply when I ran into the handrail I'd seen through the fence. It hit me square in the stomach and I would have fallen right over the top if Satan hadn't grabbed me by the back of my shirt. I looked down into a seething pit of activity. It looked as though the ground had been swallowed into a cavern of tiered seating and flashing lights. There were cinema screens every fifty feet or so down, but they stretched into the distance, down into a hole of green light. Waves of sound rolled up from deep below. I couldn't see the bottom. Satan hefted me back onto my feet. I looked across but couldn't see the far end of The Pit either. Steam shimmered up out of the middle like a wall of churning mist, which swallowed the green light.

"How far does this place go down?" I asked in wonder, "It looks like it goes forever."

"It ends about thirty miles down. The Pit is like a big ice cream cone that's been wedged into the ground. It holds over two million souls and it's always sold out, day and night for all of eternity. Lucky for us, all of the most talented people throughout history end up in Hell. Without fail, the stars of Earth become the fallen stars of Hell."

"You mean none of them go to Heaven?" I asked, perplexed.

"Well, some do eventually, but it's the nature of the business. It's a sin to make yourself into a false idol, which draws attention away from the glory of God. If you're genius enough at what you do, people will naturally worship you, it comes with the territory. That's where the myth of selling your soul comes from. If you're great in life, you must pay the price, for at least a small while. Most people revel in it, and why not? A life-time of success is worth a bit of sacrifice, don't you think?" Satan frowned for a second. "God is such a jealous, spoilt brat that he can't let anyone else have the limelight for just a second." He quickly turned his frown to a great flashy smile. "It suits me, though. This place is one of the jewels of Hell, one of the reasons I don't go insane from rage. It is a splendor of the universe, if you ask me." He waved his hand out before him. "This is The Pit!"

I could hear the noise below change and a roar of applause floated up to my ears. I admit I was curious to see what was happening down there. Suddenly, the ground started to give way beneath us. I scrambled forward, straining to reach the handrail, which was quickly slipping above us.

"Relax," Satan said calmly behind me. "We're going down to our seats, box seats mind you, fit for a king, or a dark prince." He laughed.

The earth literally swallowed the both of us whole, rocks and dirt rumbling around us in a sphere; never touching us, like we were enveloped in a bubble of air that was burrowing down into the ground. The ground stayed solid just below my feet, receding as we fell down and down into darkness, faster and faster. Just as suddenly as it had begun, we shuddered to a complete stop. There was another rumble and a hallway opened before us into an open space. The eerie green light I'd seen from above flooded through and a mass of sound cascaded towards us. It was a racket of grinding and banging and thumping, which sounded like nothing I'd ever heard.

I stopped and listened for a while longer, and the mess of sound turned into the most bizarre and beautiful music I'd ever encountered. The sounds rose and fell into light and shade, making me feel happy one moment before driving me into anger the next. It was as if I was actually feeling the same emotions as the musicians who were playing the music. The tunes rolled on as we walked through the hall into the green light. We came to a mid-sized glass room suspended twenty feet in the air and thirty feet back from the stage. I looked down. The floor was made of glass as well. I could see a crowd of moshing bodies beneath us, moving up and down with the music. There were humans and demons, all piled in together on the floor below. A fight had broken out down to the side, between a small fat man dressed in a full tuxedo and a naked demon, who was dancing provocatively to the music. The little fat man was poking the demon in the chest, shouting in his face while the demon shouted back, dancing the whole time, thrusting his hips at the man lecturing him.

I moved my eyes up into the grandstands. They stretched right up, out of sight, hundreds upon thousands of rows of seating. Every space in The Pit was crammed full. People were packed in together like cows in a cattle truck. The sound was incredible. It came from every direction. I could feel the bass shivering through my spine.

Finally, I turned to look back at the hallway from where we'd entered; it had disappeared. We were literally in a skybox, levitating in the air, encased in a glass cube. Some seats molded up from the floor beneath us. I fell into a chair which was contoured perfectly to the curves of my body. I looked across at Satan who sat enthralled, watching the stage, tapping his feet and nodding his head.

"Now, this is entertainment!" he yelled above the noise. "This is living, not like those sloths back in the lounge. You can actually learn from this spectacle and involve yourself in it. This is genius at work!"

I looked to the stage for the first time to see a pale human screaming into the air with a band of demons behind him. His arms spread wide, an impossibly high voice peeled a long stretching note, which then fell down three octaves to a raspy bass. An explosion of flames erupted behind him as the song ended and the stage fell into blackness. The crowd burst into applause. Even Satan leapt to his feet next to me, clapping his hands and whistling. He looked at me like a little kid.

"He just keeps getting better!" The Devil yelled, "I never tire of Jeff Buckley."

A spotlight shone onto the stage punctuating the darkness to reveal a figure at the microphone, holding his hands in the air pleading for silence. The crowd complied, cutting off their applause until silence rippled through the arena. The figure was dressed in tails and top hat, like a ringmaster at the circus. He leant into the microphone to speak.

"And now, ladies and gentlemen," he boomed, the sound of his voice reverberating throughout The Pit. "It's time for this evening's next spectacle. An event so gruesome, and grotesque, that it was almost banned by Satan himself."

"He's exaggerating," The Devil whispered quickly beside me, "but it's all part of the show."

I looked back to the stage as the Master of Ceremonies continued.

"This is a battle of strength, of courage, of survival. A battle to the death between two evenly matched enemies!"

The crowd jeered lightly, but subsided as the speaker held his arms up for silence once more.

"We have with us, in the black corner, the ruling champion of The Pit. He has beaten all challengers in his last one hundred nights of straight competition. During his last bout he disemboweled his opponent on stage and ate his entrails. Ladies and Gentlemen, I give you: The Destroyer of Souls, The Crusher of Spirits…"

A flame started to flicker in the far corner of the stage, lighting a black, hulking creature as it strode slowly out into the open.

"He is The Slayer of Hope, The Unforgiving Avenger of Damnation, our champion, the Demon Balthazar!"

The crowd roared as the flame behind the figure detonated. I couldn't see his face, but the Demon was gigantic, muscles bulging from every limb. He towered above the commentator by at least three feet, and was twice as wide. I pitied the poor soul who had to fight this Goliath.

"And as the challenger," the ring-master yelled above the crowd, which immediately fell silent. "We have a special treat for all this evening! Ladies and Gentlemen, he is recently dead, and fresh to the dominion of Hell, Balthazar's killer in life, and a champion in his own right. Escorting the Prince of Darkness this evening, I give you the maniac, Michael!"

TEN

I SAT UNDER THE GLARE OF THE SPOTLIGHT like a stunned deer, the halogen globes blinding me. I could barely hear the roar of the crowd over my ticking mind. Had I just heard correctly? I thought frantically. Was I to fight? And this demon was the man I'd killed on earth? My stomach constricted into a twisted knot of fear. I felt someone beside me and then I heard The Devil whisper in my ear.

"It's time to face your demons, Michael. It's time to confront yourself. This is the next step. This is the road to salvation."

I felt myself being lifted by invisible hands as I drifted slowly in the air over the crowd before the stage. I struggled and writhed around but continued down toward the howling black demon called Balthazar. The strangest thought went through my head. *I don't even know his real name.* I turned back to look above me at Satan, who just stood nodding at me, looking me in the eyes. I felt like a lamb being led to the slaughter.

My feet thumped on the stage. Balthazar roared and instantly charged at me. Luckily, I was off balance and stumbled forward as he skidded past me, bowling into a stack of speakers at the side of the stage, which scattered like Styrofoam blocks into the crowd. I had a few merciful seconds to assess my situation. There was nowhere to run to, nowhere to turn. I would have to try and fight this beast.

The hulking Balthazar picked himself up off the stage floor. He turned and walked slowly back at me, pointing.

"You sent me down here, you scum. Now it's time to feel the same pain."

I looked closely at him for the first time. His face was a deformed knot of scars wrapped around two, yellow eyes. He had no nose, just a collapsed hole where my fist had shattered his skull on earth. He wasn't even recognizable from the man I'd once fought. He truly was a Demon.

"I'm going to tear your scrawny arms out of their sockets, you little runt," he grunted as he lunged at me again. I dove to the side and rolled back to my feet, in complete survival mode. I looked around for a weapon, anything I could use. There was nothing on the stage. There was no way I would match him in brute strength. He thundered towards me again. I yelled at him, trying to buy time.

"How can you say I sent you down here? You're here for your sins, Balthazar, not just because you're dead. I only sped up the inevitable. I barely recognize you, you're like pure evil. You disgust me."

He howled in anger, lashing out and clipping my arm. I was sent spinning onto the ground, crashing to the back of the stage. My arm began throbbing, but it wasn't serious. I climbed back up again, watching as Balthazar raised his arms at the crowd, thriving on the applause. While his back was turned I searched the stage again for something, anything. There was only the microphone stand close by. I unplugged the lead attached to it and picked up the stand, ripping off the bottom to make a metal staff for myself. I yelled out to my opponent again, attacking his vanity, his pride.

"They're not cheering for you, Balthazar, they're cheering for me! No one could cheer for someone as ugly as you. You've been deformed with hate and anger. Give it up or you'll be stuck in Hell forever!"

He whirled around, seething. Balthazar stamped his foot in rage, sending a shudder through the stage. He ran towards me again, but this time I was ready. I fought back, taking him off guard. Jumping forward, I swung with all the strength in my body. I hit him square in the stomach, with a resounding smack. The metal bar ricocheted in my hands, sending vibrations up into my arms. The blow had stopped Balthazar's charge, but he didn't so much as take a backward step. The demon ripped the weapon from my grip and threw it clattering to the floor. He cackled with insane laughter and turned to the crowd again, raising his arms in the air, screaming.

"This human is no match for me, the mighty Demon Balthazar. He is nothing; he is weak!"

His words hit me: *The Demon Balthazar.* He was not the man I killed on earth. There might be some remnants of his soul inside, but this was not who he was, this was who he'd become by choice. The truth of my own words echoed in my head. *You're here for your sins, Balthazar, not just because you're dead.* It was like a weight had been lifted from me. I might have killed this man, but I was not responsible for his further damnation. That was his doing. He was evil. I felt no remorse at all for what he'd become, just pity.

I steeled myself as the demon turned around again, hate in his malaria-yellow eyes. He threw his head back and howled at the sky. Suddenly, he fell to his knees holding his ears, screaming in pain. I looked up. The boiling furnace of a guilty sky blazed above me. The whole crowd began to cry out in anguish. I collapsed.

ELEVEN

Covering my head from the view of the crowd, I crouched in my corner and pulled a small bag of cocaine out of my shorts' pocket. I placed it beneath my left nostril and inhaled sharply, sucking the powder into my lungs. I felt instantly charged. This had become my pre-fight ritual, the only time I used the drug, lest it not affect me in the desired way. It made me feel invincible, capable of anything.

I stood back up to my full height. I felt fit, lithe, fast and strong. I'd trained hard to get rid of my beer-addled body, to hone it into a sleek weapon. I rubbed my bare hands over my ribbed stomach and back up again. The enhanced sensation from the drugs made my skin tingle.

I'd flown to Thailand a month previously to compete on the underground fighting circuit in Bangkok. It was reputedly the toughest in the world and very lucrative. Since my realization that I'd wasted three years of my life behind slot machines and drowning in beer, I'd become obsessed with becoming the best fighter I could. I trained incessantly, day and night, using the skipping rope that Dante had left in my fridge as my first tool for getting back to a proper weight. Completely neurotic about my diet, my only vice had become the toot of white powder I took before my fights. I was focused and ready. I believed strongly that I had become one of the best fighters in the world, all by myself. I'd been too proud to go back to my old coach and ask for his help. I wanted to stand on my own two feet for once.

I danced into the ring, holding my arms out to the crowd, soaking in their applause. I would put on a great show for them. I would toy with this local favorite before crushing his spirits and his body. I hadn't lost a fight since coming to Thailand. I had been pushed on several occasions, but never really challenged. I hoped in my heart that I would be this time. I was ready for the fight. I began to sweat, not just from the humid Thai climate and cocaine, but also from anticipation of the challenge my opponent posed. He was much taller than me, with long legs and arms. He was fit, with quick hands and lethal feet. His name was Seuua Khrohng, which meant 'huge tiger'. Seuua's head was shaved bald, but he had thick black eyebrows that framed his Asian eyes. He smiled. He had a full set of teeth, which was rare for a Thai fighter. It was a sign of great skill.

We touched hands in the center of the ring and then retreated to our corners. I looked around as I did. We were out in the open air, behind a row of dilapidated shops in the back streets of Bangkok City. Some people sat on the roofs of the lowest buildings, watching. Steps had been cut down into the ground in a large circle around the fighting space. We stood in the center of the ring. Spectators stood on each tier, waving their Baht notes in the air, chanting "Suu, Suu, Suu… Fight, Fight, Fight!"

The referee stood in the center of the ring holding his arm in the air. Once it dropped, we would begin. There were only a couple of simple rules: no kicking, punching or biting of the groin; and stop when the other fighter goes limp. That was all. The referee dropped his arm and leapt out of the way.

I stalked into the middle of the ring, while my challenger stayed where he was, just watching me. I waited. He would come to me eventually. I looked him in the eyes. There was no fear there, just the calculation of a warrior. After a few seconds, he moved in. Jumping quickly, springing off the balls of his feet, he threw a straight punch at my face. I blocked with ease and made a low counter kick, catching him on the shins. It made a fierce slapping sound. Seuua hopped backwards again to the outer ring. I bounced from foot to foot, keeping light and ready. My opponent jumped in again, this time leading with his legs. I jumped to the side expertly. He attacked again instantly, with the same jump kick. I tried to dodge the same way, but he followed through his kick with a hard punch to my face, which sent me sprawling onto the ground. Seuua didn't relent. Straight away he jumped down, dropping a knee into my back, sending excruciating pain up my spine and into my neck. I wriggled from under him and struggled to my feet, panting. How could this local be beating me? I thought. How could he be faster and stronger than me? I was the best. I stumbled around the outside the fighting ring with spectators' breath on my back.

Seuua stood calmly in the middle of the ring, unmoving, watching me. My right knee ached. I'd fallen poorly and dropped too much weight on it. Mercifully, Seuua let me recover from his last attack. I brought my breathing under control and felt the pain in my knee subside somewhat. I launched into a fierce kicking attack, throwing my feet toward my opponent's ribs, legs and then neck. Seuua blocked each kick easily with his superior reach. I couldn't get through his defense. I hit again, looking for an opening in his guard. After a few jabs I noticed that every time I punched, he left a gap on his right side, just above his ribs. I feigned a punch, but turned and went for the gap, grunting with effort as I struck him in the side. He wheezed, as the air flew from his lungs. I hit again quickly on the other side while he was doubled over and leapt back. That's right, I thought to myself, now you know who's boss. Cocky with my minor victory, I turned to the crowd and whooped, raising an arm in the air. It was a big mistake. As soon as I raised my fist above my shoulder, I felt The Tiger's elbow in my thigh. How he'd recovered so quickly I would never know, but the blow caused me to fall. On my way to the dirt, Seuua caught me with a hit to the temple. Before I went blank, I smiled. My cockiness and my pride had been my downfall; now I had reason to be humble. I had been beaten.

TWELVE

SHAKING MY HEAD FREE OF THE VISION, I climbed to my knees. I looked up to see Balthazar still writhing on the ground. Apparently the more evil you were on the outside the more guilt you felt on the inside. He kicked and screamed, holding his head while I had time to recover. So I'd made it back to health, but I had been vain about it. I was glad that I had had humility beaten into me by someone better than me. Again, I felt sickened at seeing myself in that light, but decided it was better to learn from my youthful mistakes and use them to become a better person.

Balthazar stopped convulsing on the ground. He grunted as drool dripped from his mouth and he stood to face me.

"Michael, you should have finished me while I was helpless," he yelled. "It's what I would have done!"

"I made that mistake once before, Balthazar," I yelled back. "It cost me years of guilt. It's time to finish you the right way."

I charged at him. He roared as I got close and swung his thick black fists at my head. I let him lightly graze the crown of my head and pretended to fall to the ground in pain. He turned to the crowd again and howled in triumph, just as I had hoped. As he turned, I grabbed the microphone lead, which lay just to the left and jumped on the demon's back, wrapping it around his neck.

Balthazar's howls of triumph turned to screams of rage as he tried to fling me from his back. I wrapped the cord tighter around his neck and held on with all my strength. He raged around the stage, twisting and turning, trying to claw me off his back. I held firm. Balthazar grew weak beneath me, his movements becoming slow. He gasped and coughed as I squeezed even tighter around his neck. He dropped to his knees, and then went limp, thundering to the ground. I held on for an extra few seconds before letting go. I stood up panting. Balthazar was still breathing softly, but he was out cold. I didn't raise my fist or yell in triumph. I just looked up at Satan and said, "We're leaving." He nodded his head in assent.

THIRTEEN

"WHAT THE HELL WAS THAT ALL ABOUT?", I shouted at Satan as we tumbled back into his car.

"What do you mean?" he asked innocently.

I almost lashed out to hit him, but thought better of it.

"Tricking me into fighting Balthazar, not giving me any warning of why we were coming here or what was going to happen!"

Satan reeled on me, stabbing me in the chest with a sharp finger. It felt like I was being skewered with a knife.

"What did you expect, Michael; me to sit there and hold your hand? Nurse you through your hard times? This is Hell! It's not all rainbows and lollypops facing your demons. I'm trying to get you over to Heaven in the best way I know and, trust me, I have plenty of experience!" He started to spit as he yelled at me. "If I had warned you about what was to happen, it wouldn't have helped you one little bit. You would have probably pissed your pants on the way, worrying about what would happen and how you would feel confronting someone you killed in life! I did you a favor. I'm doing you a favor! Don't ever take that for granted."

I felt like a stupid kid. What did I expect? I didn't know, which just made it even harder. I was exhausted, drained from my ordeal. I'd been in Hell for barely a day, but it felt like an eternity. I had seen most of my life in the third person and I hated what I saw, hated who I was.

"Do I really need to give you another pep talk?" Satan asked, switching back to a casual demeanor with such ease it made me blink. He was a chameleon, there was no doubt.

"I tell you what," he said. "Let's go and have some fun and take a break. I'll take you to Magdalene's Mansion."

I remembered the name from looking down at Hell on the top floor of Satan's building. It was a brothel.

"I don't think so," I said flatly, not taking to the idea.

"Why not?" he asked, digging me in the ribs. "It's all fun, Michael, just a bit of play. You don't owe anyone anything. Let's go and blow off some steam."

"What about lust? Isn't that a sin?" I replied.

Satan threw his head back in the air and laughed.

"Ha! Only if your lust leads to acts like incest, rape or adultery. Sex is the most natural thing in the world, Michael. God invented it. How can he hold it against you if you want to do it as often as possible? Even I want to do it, it's so much fun, and I'm not even human."

"But a brothel?" I argued. "It just seems wrong."

"Worse than tricking a woman into sleeping with you by making her think you're a nice guy, and then leaving in the morning?" he asked. "Worse than masturbating in the dark with your eyes closed and your ears open? I think not. At least there's no trickery with a brothel. I know what I'm getting and so do they: money. It's a fair trade and believe me, the girls at Mary's enjoy what they do; there's no need for them to do it. There are plenty of other ways to get by down here. Come on, at least to have a look."

I gave in. What was the point in resisting The Devil? He had me.

"Great!" Satan clapped his hands together and banged on the divider-screen in the car with his fist. "To Mary's, driver. My treat."

We sped up abruptly, heading back toward the suburb of Smoking Gun.

FOURTEEN

WE WALKED THROUGH THE DOORS of the biggest brothel I could have ever imagined: Magdalene's Mansion. The building must have been over one hundred stories high, made completely of red glazed glass with a detailed painting of a naked woman holding a whip drawn on the façade.

Satan led the way over the red carpet interior, toward the reception desk. It was manned by the most stunning, auburn haired goddess I had ever laid eyes on. She was wearing a sheer, black negligee that was completely see-through and clinging to every curve of her perfect body. Despite myself, I couldn't keep my eyes off her.

She looked up with light green eyes, smiling as she recognized who I was with.

"Well, hello there, Mr. Asmodeus," she beamed with a shining smile of straight, white teeth. "It's been too long since you've walked through those doors!"

"Much too long!" Satan smiled, leaning over the counter to kiss her on the cheek. "How have you been, Oba my love? Keeping busy?"

She giggled at his kiss. "Oh, you know we're always busy. Almost as busy as you. I assume you want to see Madam Magdalene?"

"I do, Oba, you know me so well! I don't need to be shown up, I know the way. Could you please look after my man, Michael, here. He wasn't too keen on coming, he's shy, but by the look in his eyes maybe you could change his mind?" He winked. Oba laughed seductively, facing me for the first time.

"Oh, I'm sure I can manage him," she purred, looking me up and down.

"I'll meet you back at my office," Satan said over his shoulder as he walked towards a side hallway. "I'll leave my car out the front for you. Have a good time!"

He disappeared from view. I looked back to Oba and blushed. She was truly gorgeous, a goddess. I didn't know where to look, afraid my eyes would just stare at her naked body beneath the diaphanous negligee. I ended up staring at my feet. She laughed.

"Oh, come now, Michael," she pouted, lifting my chin and forcing me to look into her eyes. "I won't bite," she whispered, "unless you want me to."

"I don't want you to do anything to me," I lied, keeping my line of sight above her shoulders. I could feel blood fill my cheeks, among other things. I needed a distraction. "Tell me about this place," I asked. "How many people work here?"

"Very well," she sighed, "if you really want to be boring, let's go for a walk."

She took me by the hand and led me down the passage that Satan had disappeared down just a few moments earlier. Her skin felt warm and soft against my palm. I ached to press myself against her, but I fought the urge. I couldn't shake the feeling that this was wrong.

"This is Magdalene's Mansion," Oba started in a seductive tone, "where all of your deepest desires are brought to life. We cater for everyone here, every fantasy, every need. We tickle, suck, lick and delight. We whip, smack, tease and bite. We can be soft or rough. We'll beg to please you or demand you to please us. Chains are in the dungeon and orgies are upstairs. There's everything else on the levels in between. In total, a hundred and twenty floors of sexual pleasure. We have over ten thousand girls in our employ and almost as many men -- if that's the way you swing."

Oba stopped and opened a door. Around ten sweaty bodies writhed on the ground in a blue room, full of cushions. A blonde near the doorway looked up as a demon thrust into her

55

from behind. She looked me in the eyes and moaned, "Mmm, won't you come and join us?"

I stepped back and Oba shut the door.

"There is nothing we won't do for you, Michael, nothing. We're here to serve you, our desire is for you."

We continued down the hall, peeking into many doors as we went. There were rooms with swimming pools, beds, dunes of sand and mock prisons. Some rooms had guests and others were empty. My mind boggled as I peered into this world of absolute hedonism.

Finally, Oba led me into an empty room that was softly lit with a large bed in the middle. She walked in ahead of me and turned as she fell onto the bed. She peeled the negligee off her beautiful body and motioned for me to join her.

"Come on, Michael," she smiled. "You know you want to. Give in to your desires, they're only natural."

I stayed put, looking at her, fighting every fiber of my being not to jump onto the bed with Oba and take her. My resolve weakened as she started to rub her breasts in front of me, sliding her hand down between her parting legs. Slowly, she stopped and looked at me. I went to open my mouth to apologize, but she leaned forward and grabbed my shirt, pulling me on top of her. Pressing her hot lips into mine, her tongue snaked and swirled inside my mouth. I drew in her scent. It reminded me of something, or someone. I fell onto the bed looking into Oba's eyes. Slowly they turned from her light green shade to the most exquisite blue, like a vision.

FIFTEEN

The plane rumbled around us through jolting turbulence. The seatbelt light flashed on. The beautiful girl next to me grabbed my arm for support. She looked up at me, and I stared into her impossibly big, blue eyes. She started and jumped back into her seat. "Oh, I'm so sorry," she gasped and went red with embarrassment, taking her hands off my arm.

"It's fine," I said soothingly. It had been a very long time since I had seen such a naturally beautiful woman. There wasn't a trace of vanity in the way she held herself, and such trusting eyes.

"First time flying?" I asked.

"Second," she admitted. "I've just been on holiday with my friends in Thailand, and I'm on my way home. They're all going on to Australia."

Her tension eased as the turbulence subsided and we started to make small talk.

"I'm Charlotte," she said holding out her hand. I shook it lightly.

"Michael," I replied.

"Were you on holidays in Thailand too, Michael?" she asked sweetly.

I thought about lying but when I looked into her face, I couldn't. It was strange, I'd never felt this way around a woman before. Normally I was confident and brash.

"No, I was fighting in some tournaments in Bangkok," I said, looking out the window, sure she would stop talking to me after she found out what I did for a living.

"Wow!" she said.

I looked back, surprised. Rather than being frightened, she was intrigued.

"Is that how you got that big bruise on your face? I'm sorry I was staring at it before." She blushed.

"Oh, I didn't notice," I stammered.

She had been staring at me, my heart skipped a little. I felt like such a dork with her sitting there next to me.

"Did you do well in the fights?" She asked.

"Not my last one, the other guy beat me up pretty good." I said. "But I get paid either way."

"So you let other men beat you up for money?" she teased.

"It's not like that," I protested, "I actually quite enjoy it; fighting, anyway, not the losing part."

"Enjoy fighting?" she asked. "How do you enjoy it?"

"Fighting has always been an outlet for me to escape," I told her.

It's funny the things you will say to a complete stranger.

"I enjoy inflicting pain on other fighters because they remind me of everything I don't like about myself. I guess I'm a bit of a thug, but so are the men I fight. I love showing I have power over them."

"That's so interesting!" she said, looking at me without a trace of revulsion.

I couldn't believe it. She was so open to what I had to say, so perfect, nodding along with understanding.

"And what about you, Charlotte?" I asked, after talking about myself for a few minutes. "What do you do with yourself when you're not on holiday in Thailand?"

"I've just finished my nursing degree at college and I have a placement at the UCSF Children's Hospital in San Francisco."

It was my turn to be interested. She was beautiful, smart and giving.

"So you'd be able to patch me up after a fight?" I joked.

She laughed. Before I knew it, the wheels of our plane had screeched onto the tarmac in Los Angeles. We'd talked the entire time without a break. I had opened up to her in ways that I never had with anyone before. It was the first time I'd really talked to someone. Not just about what I do, but my feelings. I was giving her a part of myself without even knowing I was doing it. There was not a doubt in my mind that I'd fallen for this girl. We walked together off the plane but had to part ways at the transfer desk. I stopped awkwardly, wanting to say something smart and ask her for her number. I couldn't get the words out, but she saved me.

"So will I see you again, Michael?" Charlotte asked with her innocent smile.

"Of course," I grinned. I was so excited. She wanted to see me again just as much as I wanted to see her.

SIXTEEN

I BLINKED. I was looking into green eyes with soft lips pressed against mine. I jumped back.

"What? Charlotte?" But I was looking at the prostitute, Oba.

"Relax," she said. "You're with Oba now." She tried to lean in but I stopped her. I stood up off the bed.

"I'm sorry, Oba. I'm spoken for."

She looked hurt. "Well, why follow me in here in the first place, then?" she asked, her hands on her hips.

"No, I didn't know. I…" I didn't even finish my sentence. I turned and walked from the room with Oba yelling for me to come back, but my interest in such a gorgeous woman had died with my regained memory of Charlotte.

I had to find Satan. I had to find out about the rest of my life. Did I ever see Charlotte again? I must have, I knew it; she was 'the one'. She must be. Why else would I have had a vision of her? I was happy, nervous and scared all at the same time. Just to have been in the presence of someone so truly wonderful had been a reprieve from the rest of my life. What if I didn't get to see her again? Who knows what could have happened; I was living in Las Vegas and she was in San Francisco. Could I have turned into a stalker or something? I doubted it. I would never do anything to hurt my Charlotte. It sounded crazy, me thinking of her as *my* Charlotte, but somehow I knew that we must have ended up together. I was certain.

I burst through the front doors of the brothel and onto the street. My focus was so intense that I didn't even feel the heat of the outside air. I flung the door of the waiting limousine open and pounded on the divider window. "Take me to Satan," I yelled. We peeled out into the traffic. I sat forward in my seat, smiling. "I met the love of my life," I said aloud. I was so happy. There was no way I was staying down in Hell with so much love in my heart. I would do no wrong, hurt no soul nor envy any man while I had Charlotte. I was ready to see out my fate and cross over to Heaven. I would wait patiently for Charlotte to meet me there. I hoped she was okay, not too worried or sad that I'd left her alone. I smiled again. Everything would turn out fine; we would be together again eventually. Of that I was sure.

I didn't even let the car stop completely before jumping out onto the pavement. I rushed into the foyer of the building I had started the day in.

Clytemnestra still sat at reception in her black dress. She stood up, flashing her fang-like teeth in a forced smile.

"Hello, Michael," she said. "Where is Mr. Asmodeus?"

"He's not back yet?" I asked hurriedly.

"He's not with you?" she asked back with a puzzled frown.

"No, we got split up after going to The Pit." I answered cautiously. No use in getting on the wrong side of Satan; who knew what kind of a relationship he had with this woman. She glared up at me suspiciously.

"He said to meet him back here if we were separated. Should I wait for him upstairs?" I suggested, not wanting to stand under Clytemnestra's accusing eyes any longer.

"I suppose you can," she answered slowly. "Go up to the top floor. I'll send him up as soon as he arrives."

"He won't be too long," I offered confidently as I walked towards the elevator, thoughts of Charlotte racing through my head.

The elevator doors opened and I stepped inside, pressing floor 666. As the elevator jerked upward, I leaned back and sighed. I closed my eyes and pictured Charlotte's innocent face, her gorgeous smile and her throaty laugh. She was the epitome of natural beauty. I hoped deep in my bones that we had met again after that day. I had the feeling we had, but was nervous with uncertainty. I switched back and forth from being confident

60

that we were destined to be together to being completely unsure of anything. I was afraid that I might have let a once in a lifetime moment slip through my foolish fingers.

The elevator doors slid open onto the top level and I walked into the lushly carpeted room. The view was incredible. Despite the thoughts pounding through my brain, I was once again awestruck at the savage beauty of Hell. The sprawling city set against the jagged mountain, deserts and lakes was stunning. All the most incredible landscapes of earth rolled into a supernatural setting of eerie light and construction. I took a seat on the floor near the furthest window, watching the traffic below. It was still hard to accept that existence of the soul really did go on after death. I had never fully believed in the afterlife and now it was being rammed down my throat.

Absentmindedly, I was playing with something on my finger as I thought about Charlotte. I looked down at my hand. On my left, a sparkling gold band sat on my ring finger. My heart stopped beating for just a moment. I couldn't understand why I hadn't noticed it before. I had been so caught up with the events of the day that I hadn't taken in this simple, but important clue to my previous life. Was this a wedding ring? I cast my eyes out to the horizon to see what I was now impatient for: a boiling flame rolling across the skyscape. A flare of light shot across the clouds with a loud roar. I lay back ready for my next vision.

SEVENTEEN

The cold sand crinkled beneath my toes as we walked along the beach, Charlotte's petite hand clasped in mine. Brilliant stars twinkled in the cloudless sky. I inhaled the warm night air.

"This is so romantic, isn't it?" Charlotte smiled next to me, giving my hand a light squeeze. "I can't believe we're in Greece, it's just so wonderful, Michael."

I laughed at her enthusiasm. She was always so happy, so positive. I loved how it rubbed off onto me. I was glad to be alive for the first time ever. I looked forward to waking up in the morning because she was with me. Charlotte had been my savior, my guiding light since we'd met by chance on a plane from Thailand. We'd fallen for each other quickly; me with her kind heart and giving nature and her with my determination. She said I inspired her. I felt so wanted around her, so needed. She made me want to be a better person. I had given away the underground fights in Las Vegas and moved with her to San Francisco to become a personal trainer. I even ran some boxing classes at a gym near our apartment in North Beach and trained some homeless kids for free. It felt good to be giving something back, creating something instead of just tearing people down.

Charlotte loved her job at the hospital, taking care of children. She worked long and hard hours. Often, she had heart-breaking stories of young children with leukemia or horrible burns, but somehow she always came home with a smile on her face. Charlotte had a knack for seeing the silver lining in any situation, which might have explained how she could love a man with my past.

We came to the end of the beach and flopped down on the sand, looking up at the brilliant sky.

"Isn't it amazing?" I asked. "You know the sky in the northern hemisphere is different to the sky in the southern hemisphere? They have completely different stars and constellations."

"How does an ex-fighter know so much about the stars?" she asked, baffled. She was constantly amazed at my knowledge of pointless things.

I shrugged. "I guess I read too many books," I said.

"No, I love it!" she said, hitting me on the arm playfully. "So, Mr. Know-it-All," she teased. "Do you know anything about the stars up there, or are you just pretending to be smart?"

"Well, actually," I smiled, "I do know one story about one of the constellations up there, Lotte." She giggled at my nickname for her.

"Tell me," she commanded, lying on her back, pulling me down next to her so we had our heads side by side. We peered up into the heavens.

"Okay," I said. "Do you see that group of stars straight up there?" I pointed and she looked along my finger.

"I think so," she squinted. "The one with the four bright ones all in a row?"

"That's the one," I answered. "Well, that is one of the first constellations ever recognized in history. It's called Andromeda, named after a beautiful princess who lived in ancient Greece. She was the daughter of the King Cepheus and his queen, Cassiopeia. In fact, Andromeda was so beautiful that her mother Cassiopeia would gloat to other people that she was even more stunning than the Nereids, nymph daughters of the sea god, Nereus."

Charlotte snuggled into me as I continued my story.

"Now, unfortunately for the Queen, the Nereids overheard her bragging of Andromeda's beauty and complained to Poseidon, the God of the Sea. They demanded that Cassiopeia be punished for her pride. Poseidon agreed, so he summoned a terrible sea monster called Cetus and commanded him to lay waste to the lands over which Andromeda's parents ruled. He told Cetus to take the form of a monstrous whale and to kill people and cattle who dared go near the sea. Cetus did as he was told and set to his task of destruction, slaughtering many up and down the coast. King Cepheus had a duty to protect his people; they begged him to save them from the terror of Cetus. So, the King consulted an oracle who could communicate with the gods when men sought their advice. The oracle told Cepheus that there was only one way to stop the slaughter, to offer his daughter Andromeda as a sacrifice."

"No," Charlotte gasped. "He didn't do it, did he?"

"He had no choice," I said theatrically, enjoying the fact that she was so enrapt in the tale. "King Cepheus was bound to protect his subjects. He made the bitter choice to chain his precious daughter to the rocks, and then abandoned her to await the terrible Cetus. When the monster saw Andromeda chained up, he left his wrathful destruction of the coast and *began swimming towards the ledge where she was trapped, so he could devour her.*

"Oh no!" Charlotte cried.

"Suddenly," I continued, "a distant figure appeared in the sky. It was Perseus, the courageous son of Zeus and Danae. He was returning from a quest where he had slain the dreaded Medusa. As Perseus passed over the coast, he looked down and saw Cetus swimming toward the chained maiden, Andromeda. He jumped down to the girl's aid and was instantly overwhelmed by her beauty. 'Why are you thus bound?' he asked her, to which Andromeda explained Perseus the story of her boastful mother and the jealous Nereids. Perseus quickly found King Cepheus and told him that he could save his daughter from the monster Cetus, but in return he demanded Andromeda's hand in marriage and a kingdom for them to rule together. The King immediately agreed, for he loved his daughter dearly. Perseus leapt down into the ocean and attacked the monster Cetus. With the first thrust of his mighty sword, Perseus found the soft piece of flesh between Cetus' armored scales and stabbed him in the heart, killing him.

Elated, King Cepheus and Cassiopeia led Perseus and Andromeda to their house, where a great feast and celebration took place. Andromeda and Perseus were married and lived a long and happy life together. Later when they died, they were rewarded by the gods and given their own place together in the sky. See just to the right of those stars. That's Perseus in the sky; he watches over his wife in the heavens."

"That's just beautiful," Charlotte beamed.

"And see that star over there?" I asked.

"Which one?" she replied inquisitively, looking into the night sky.

"This one," I said, holding up the diamond ring I'd been keeping in my pocket the whole time we'd been on the beach. "This is your star, Lotte. Will you marry me?"

Tears filled her eyes as she looked from the ring to me. I started to cry as well, despite trying to hold it back.

"Of course I will, Michael," she sobbed. "I love you so much."

I pushed the ring onto her finger and she threw her arms around my neck, pushing me back into the sand, showering me with kisses. I was the happiest man alive.

EIGHTEEN

I LAY ON THE CARPET in Satan's building, holding on to the vision I'd just witnessed. I savored every moment, every detail of Charlotte and my proposal to her. I replayed it again and again in my mind, twirling the wedding ring on my finger.

"I'm in heaven," I said out loud.

"Actually, you're still in Hell for now," The Devil boomed as the elevator doors opened and he strode into the room, "at least for a few more hours yet." He smiled holding his arms open, like he was welcoming a dear friend.

"I'm in love!" I said, laughing as I got up and walked towards him.

"With Oba?" The devil asked.

"Who?" I replied, puzzled.

"I'm kidding!" he smiled. "This is The Devil you're talking to, Michael. I know you're in love with Charlotte, your wife.

"You know?" I asked. "But why didn't you tell me about any of this? Why go through all of the pain if you knew I would choose to go to Heaven without so much as a second thought? This whole day has been a waste of time."

"There you go again, Michael," The Devil said with a tutting noise. "You second guess my methods. Remember this is a process. You needed to find out slowly who you were, somewhat equivalent to being drip-fed your life. Otherwise, it is too much to take in, too much to handle. Your joy at knowing Charlotte is partly defined by your suffering. You love her so much because of what you've been through, and the fact that she accepts you despite what you feel about yourself deep down.

"So, she really does love me?" I asked.

"Of course," Satan replied. "You just saw it with your own eyes."

I would never have believed it a few hours ago, but all of my suffering, all of my downfalls had been wiped away by meeting one person. I didn't think I deserved it. Maybe I didn't.

"And I didn't mess things up? I didn't ruin it like everything else?"

I was suddenly worried that maybe I'd done something to hurt her or change her mind about me.

"You were happily married right up until the moment you died," Satan said. He had just confirmed it! We were married, happily. I was ecstatic.

"Is she okay without me there?" I asked, thinking now only of Charlotte.

Satan turned around pointing to the sky, which started to boil and burn on the horizon once again.

"Better to show you than to tell you," he said. "It's time to see how you died."

NINETEEN

Screams. All I could hear were the screams of Charlotte. They were not defiant, but defeated wails of suffering. It was as if hope had been torn from her soul and ripped apart, then stuffed into her throat, gagging her. I couldn't move. I must've been hit from behind as soon as we entered our apartment. I blinked the blood from my eyes. I was on the floor, sprawled out, legs twisted. My spine felt as if it had been shattered. Limp arms hung out in front of me, teasing me with how useless they were. I'd made a living fighting with those arms; they still looked strong, but they were dead.

I looked to where I could hear Charlotte. My beautiful wife was hanging from the wall by two metal spikes, driven through each shoulder. She was bruised and beaten, now just sobbing. Red spit hung from her bottom lip, dribbling down past her feet to the ground. How she was still conscious I had no idea. Blood dripped from between her legs. She had been raped, her humanity stolen from her by some vile creature. What monster had done this to the woman I love?

She stopped crying and looked up, right into my eyes, glassy with tears.

"I love you," she whispered, weakly.

With that, a fist came out from the side of my vision and punched her in the face, crunching her fragile bones back into her brain with a sickening crack. She was dead.

I didn't even yell. I was silent. Bloody tears rolled from my eyes, the rage bubbling inside me.

"You'll pay for this," I croaked.

Laughter. Not from one person, but a few. I could see only him. The one who killed Lotte. He smiled at me with perfect shiny teeth and clear blue eyes. Blonde, wavy hair framed a handsome, adolescent face. He looked barely seventeen. His smooth chin had no trace of a man who needed to shave. His dimpled cheeks pinched into a grin.

"Do you even realize how ridiculous that sounds?" he said in a nasal voice. "You can't even move, let alone stand up and face me, you dirty fool." He bent down and put his nose an inch from mine. "I raped her for God," he sneered.

I lurched forward and sunk my teeth into the tip of his pretty little nose, ripping through the flesh and tearing a chunk completely off. I spat it back into his shocked face as he fell backwards onto the floor, yelping in pain.

"You taste like evil," I rasped, his blood seeping from my mouth. "She never hurt a soul, you pig, you're pathetic."

"You're the one who is evil, you piece of scum!" he yelled, holding his nose as dark red blood oozed between his fingers, like muck from a sewer.

"God has asked us to send you to Hell, Michael. Where you belong! He wants you to burn down there for your sins. You killed her by knowing her."

"You're sick," I panted, stunned at his words. "You're insane. God? What are you talking about? You don't make sense. You're just a twisted psychopath who breaks into the houses of innocent people to torture them."

He sneered again, the blood staining his teeth crimson.

"I make sense!" he boomed as he scrambled back to his feet. "I make perfect sense. You're just too thick to see the truth."

He walked back to where Lotte's limp body was hanging on the wall, and lifted her shattered face. He pressed his cheek against hers, their faces side by side looking at me. Her lifeless eyes stared through me, while his bored into my soul.

"If you had never met this pretty little thing, she would still be alive." He looked back at her in disgust and dropped her head so it flopped back down on her chest.

"What are you talking about? You're crazy," I repeated, unable to comprehend what he was saying.

He wiped the blood off his hands onto her blouse and turned back to face me.

"No, I'm not." He said. "I'm God's messenger and God doesn't want trash like you mixing with his more beautiful creations. Your tainted fate mixed with hers and it killed her. The Lord doesn't want her in Heaven now that you've been with her, and he's angry at you for ruining an innocent. You killed her by being so selfish that you had to have her in your life, even when you knew deep down that it would end in death."

I had been a fool, I thought. I'd dreamt of my violent death many nights for most of my life, right up until the point that I'd met her. Then the nightmares had stopped.

"I thought she had saved me," I whispered to myself.

Charlotte's murderer began to laugh again.

68

"Ohhh, that's sad," he said in a mocking tone. "It was the other way around, Michael. You dragged her into sin. You've compromised her purity, twisted her perception of what is good and evil. How could she accept that you had hurt others if she wasn't blinded by her love for you?"

All I could do was stare my hatred at him. Bare, cold hatred. He looked in my eyes and actually took a step back. This was a murderer standing before me, plain and simple. He must have stalked us to know so much about our lives. How could this be happening to me? To us? I struggled to make sense of it. There was no reason for this.

Charlotte's killer looked over to his left and clicked his fingers. Someone handed him a white suit-jacket and said, "I kept it clean like you asked me to, Gideon."

So this despicable creature has a name, I thought. I will never forget it. Gideon.

As he slid his jacket on, Gideon looked back at me.

"The Brethren have done their job, Michael," he said. "We are delivering you to Hell in the name of God the Elemental."

He formed the sign of the cross over his chest and took a pill from his pocket, shoving it in my mouth. He held it shut as the pill dissolved on my tongue.

"You'll be dead in a minute. Say hello to Satan for us."

I choked and coughed as he stood up and strode from the room, laughing. Other feet shuffled out behind him. The bitter taste of poison lingered on my tongue like a chemical burn.

And there I lay, holding onto life like a half-drowned child clinging to the branches of a tree in the middle of a flooded river. The murky waters of eternity were ripping me from my pain into the dark unknown. As the light faded from my eyes I looked up at my love and had one last thought.

'I will have revenge on this monster called Gideon and his followers. He'll rot in Hell with me to torture him for the rest of existence.' Then all went dark and the river of death washed over my broken body.

PART TWO
REVELATION

ONE

MY EYES SNAPPED OPEN. I realized immediately that I was back in Hell. I felt no physical pain but I was in agony. All I'd ever cared about had been taken from me in the name of God, by a raving lunatic and some people who called themselves 'The Brethren'. It made no sense. I was nobody, an orphan who had made a living from illegal kickboxing fights, saved from a life of anger and solitude by an extraordinary girl called Charlotte.

Why would they kill me? Why would they kill her? Despite these questions, the searing reality remained: they had done it. Strangely, I became calm. I would be able to take revenge on Gideon. I would be able to make him suffer as he made my Lotte suffer, and I would find out why he did it.

"Charlotte!" I blurted, suddenly more aware. "Where is she?"

Satan looked up sleepily from the corner of the room. He sat with his legged crossed on a padded chair, with a book in his lap.

"You're back," he yawned.

"Where's Charlotte?" I repeated.

"Not here," he said.

"I want to see her!" I shouted, lunging at Satan. I grabbed his windpipe trying to crush it with my bare hands as I tripped him down to the ground.

"Oh stop," he said wearily from beneath me, not even making a move to fight back. I squeezed harder, trying to inflict some of the pain I felt onto him.

"You can't go to see her any more than I can," he continued in a steady voice. "She is trapped in limbo. She has no sins to forgive, so she is not in Hell. However, because of how she died, the violence of it, her soul lies in sorrow at the gates of Heaven. She will stay in limbo waiting for what happened to her to be made right again. She cannot go inside until the people who sinned against her lie in Hell themselves. They must accept their actions as evil and deliberate, or at least feel 'The Guilt' for having killed both of you. Only then will her soul be free."

My thoughts quickened. Her soul was in limbo, lost, waiting for me. I would do whatever it took to be with her again.

"How can I see her?" I asked frantically, pushing ever harder on his throat with no effect.

"There is a way," Satan replied. "But right now all you want is vengeance, and you must remember that revenge is a sin. Think about how it works, Michael. Until you no longer want to commit sin, you'll not be allowed near the hallowed gates or Charlotte. You will remain in Hell until your soul is clean."

A rage was building inside me, I needed to make things right before I lost control. I had to get out of Hell; I had to get back at Gideon for what he had done.

"What do I do?" I asked hurriedly. "How do I see Charlotte?"

"You must bring Gideon to justice," Satan answered slowly. "You cannot just forgive what he did, what they did." He sighed. "Once those responsible for her death are down here where they belong, then your need for revenge will be satisfied. Only then will you no longer feel the need to sin. Then, and only then, will you be able to see Charlotte. Now get off me."

He waved his hand and I sailed back across the room like a paper plane, hammering into the far wall and sliding to the floor. The impact jolted me back to my senses and I composed myself. Shaking my head clear, I got back to my feet. My wife might have been taken from me, but there was hope that I could see her again. She was not lost to me forever and that thought gave me some comfort. I knew what had to be done: avenge Lotte. I would do it, with The Devil on my side.

"That's right, my boy!" Satan exclaimed, "I am on your side, and we're a team." He walked over to me and slid his arm around my shoulders. "Together, we will avenge Charlotte."

There was still a burning question in my mind. I pushed myself away from Satan. I needed to know the truth.

"Gideon said to me just before he murdered me that he had been sent by God to kill us. Could that be true? Could he have been sent by God?"

Satan looked down to his feet in silence.

"Could he?" I roared. Satan looked up at me again with hate in his eyes.

"God is capable of murder just like everyone else, Michael," he said. "I don't know for sure, but yes, God could have sent Gideon to kill you. God will often reach down with his powerful hand and alter the lives of his creations. He does sometimes make judgment on souls before they die. If he thought you had tainted a soul he considered pure, I wouldn't put it past him to destroy you both."

I almost lashed out at Satan again for what he was telling me, but he continued before I could react.

"One thing I definitely know is that this Gideon believes that he is God's messenger. He has been bragging to his followers that he is God's confidant, that he does God's work on earth. He also believes that he is the keeper of a terrible secret that could destroy God forever."

Something clicked in my mind; a big missing piece of the jigsaw had fallen out of Satan's mouth. So, this was why Satan was helping me. He was really just using me to help himself. He didn't care about me, about Charlotte. Satan wanted Gideon. He wanted this secret. I was a pawn in a larger game.

"This is true, Michael," Satan conceded quickly. "You are a convenient ally for me, but does it make any difference? You're always part of a bigger picture. It's how you paint your individual story that makes all the difference. If Gideon is telling the truth, and God *has* instructed him to kill you because you have tainted Charlotte's soul, then you have even more reason to help me destroy both of them. The truth is, I don't know why Gideon killed you, but that doesn't change what he did. Charlotte's soul is in limbo because of him, and you have a chance to make it right. I can help you do this."

Satan was right, of course. I didn't care if he was using me. I should count myself lucky he wanted Gideon in Hell as much as I did. I could bring him to justice because I had the power and knowledge of Satan on my side.

"That's right," The Devil said, interrupting my thoughts again. "You have my knowledge and my influence. I can help you to learn powers down here that will transcend all realms. I can guide you to demons who will lead you on the path to avenging Charlotte, demons who are almost as powerful as I!"

"The powers of other demons?" I asked. "What about your powers?"

"You forget," Satan said, tapping his temple. "My powers don't translate onto earth. Once I leave Hell my talents are minimal. I can only change form and read minds. I cannot govern the same forces of nature that I can down here."

"But how will other demons' powers work on earth if yours cannot?" I asked.

"Because all of the demons in Hell were once from earth, they are *of* the earth if you like, so their powers originate from there. They have simply had the time to learn how to use their skills properly down here. Some have had thousands of years and the greatest teachers in existence helping them to amass their dark tricks. Many of their talents are unique and terrifying, even I cannot mimic them."

"You say some are almost as powerful as you. Why should they help me? What do they have to gain from helping someone so insignificant?"

The devil thought for a moment, looking in the distance for an answer that didn't seem to be there. For a full minute he stood, thinking. He finally turned to me with a plastic smile.

"Remember who you are talking to here, Michael. I am the ruler of this place; you have my name in your corner; it will hold a lot of weight to many."

"But not all?" I pushed.

"No, not all," he said, the smile fading to a snarl. "You can't expect me to hand everything to you on a platter. You'll have to sacrifice or pay something to get the power you'll need. I will help all I can, Michael, but in the end it will have to be you who helps yourself. I'm too busy running this paradise to give all my energy to you. That is, after all, my true purpose for being here. I am here to rehabilitate the damned, and help find them a way to Heaven. I'm in the soul laundering business. The Armageddon thing is something I believe will make things better for us in the future. I cannot neglect the present, lest my plans fail and Hell becomes too over populated to manage efficiently."

I began to feel afraid, scared that the Devil would be of no help at all and that I'd never be able to see Charlotte again.

"Oh come now, Michael," Satan said, sounding like a wounded star. "I have one thing in particular that will be very helpful indeed."

"Really?" I said, doubtful. "And what's that?"

"This!" he said flourishing his fingers over his palm as an apple appeared in his hand. "Knowledge, dear boy! The fruit of which will help you on your quest for revenge!"

TWO

"DON'T YOU REMEMBER YOUR BIBLE CLASS from the orphanage, Michael?" The Devil taunted, tossing the apple toward me.

I caught it and looked in my hands. It was gone. I looked up and Satan grinned as he twisted three apples in one hand, like crystal balls. I stood transfixed at how the apples spun, as if floating around his palm. I did remember bible class.

"You fed Eve the fruit of knowledge in The Garden of Eden," I said, as if in a trance.

"No, I did not," he snapped, jerking me out of my daze from watching the spinning fruit in his hand. "Eve ate it herself. I just *tempted* her to do it. You see, when God created 'man' he gave you the potential of intellect. He didn't necessarily want you to become intelligent, because intelligence leads to questions, which is what got me exiled from Heaven to Hell -- questioning his authority." Satan's eyes flashed in anger, but he continued. "Now, God put all the right chemicals there inside the brain, they just needed one final catalyst. This last ingredient happened to be inside the fruit of knowledge.

"He..." Satan said, pointing his clawed finger toward the sky, "conveniently put this fruit onto a tree in the middle of The Garden and then told Adam and Eve not to eat it. A sick mind game if you ask me. Why the hell would you put it there in the first place if you didn't want them to eat it? Why wouldn't you just *not* put it there?" He didn't give me time to respond. "God was testing his creations to see if his other grand gift to you worked. The cracker of a present I like to call Free Will: The luxury to choose what you do and don't do.

"See, God believed you would make the right choice, according to him anyway, and not eat the fruit. What an idiot!

Temptation is a powerful thing, especially to the ignorant. Ironic, that if they'd been smarter they probably wouldn't have listened to me and eaten the fruit, which, by the way, wasn't a freaking apple!"

The apples in Satan's hand instantly turned to silver orbs of light, pulsating luminance up his arm. The fruit now looked amazing, like little tasty moons levitating in his palm.

"That's right," Satan laughed. "He even made the fruit look attractive, all the incentive in the world to give it a try. Just a little poke from me, in the guise of a serpent, and Eve scoffed one of these bad boys down like a cop eating a donut! Bam!"

The Devil clicked his fingers and a thunder clap erupted about our heads, rolling through the air.

"She became *aware*. Aware of good, aware of evil, aware of her nudity and aware of Adam's. She then talked Adam into eating the fruit and he learnt also. With the knowledge of good and evil, came the knowledge of sin. They had sinned by eating the fruit. God had told them not to and they had disobeyed his word. God became so furious that he kicked them out of paradise into the deadly, real world.

"Adam grew resentful of Eve, angry that she had talked him into tasting the fruit which led to their exile from Eden. Adam, the idiot, didn't accept that he actually made the decision to eat it of his own freewill. He blamed Eve for his failure. In turn, Eve grew bitter with Adam for blaming her. They were both angry, hating each other but unable to separate for fear of dying. God had given them no knowledge of the afterlife. Soon their hate and anger turned into another emotion, another 'sin'. Lust! Adam's awareness of Eve's glorious nudity led to sinful, lusty urges to have sex with her, despite the fact he loathed her with every fiber of his being. He knew having sex with Eve despite his hate was wrong, but he did it anyway. Knowledge begot sin, for if you don't know you are doing wrong, how can it be a real sin?

"Eve felt the same lustful urges, because it was the dawn of time and no-one had invented football to keep the mind off sex! So, they fucked, a lot. Then came the babies: Cain, Abel and the rest. The birth of the human race through carnal sin. So really, if you think about it, by tempting Eve to eat that fruit I am largely responsible for humanity as we know it!"

Satan giggled again, looking at my disbelieving expression.

"What?" he asked. "Doesn't that make perfect sense?"

He was right, I couldn't really argue with him.

"Anyway," Satan pressed on. "I've gone off on a tangent and now we are back to how I can help you. Knowledge!"

He handed me one of the plump, moon-like fruits. This time it remained solid in my hand.

"I can give you the knowledge of who you want revenge on, knowledge of how to gain the power to defeat them, and knowledge of how to find out that dirty little secret about God." He smiled. "It seems we're all after a little bit of knowledge."

I closed my eyes and bit into the fruit. Waves of pleasure shuddered through my tongue and into my body. It was the best taste I'd ever experienced, the taste of power. I waited for the waves of pleasure to stop, and the wave of knowledge to begin. As the feeling subsided, I waited with eyes closed for the thoughts to come and The Devil roared with laughter. I opened my eyes and he was rolling on the ground in stitches. I stood above him, my hands on my hips waiting for his laughter to die. He eventually stopped. Wiping a tear from his eye, he chuckled.

"Since when did actual knowledge come from a piece of fruit? I told you that it simply contained a chemical that helped Adam and Eve become aware. Since then, that chemical has been passed down genetically from them to you -- through a very long line of incest, might I add. You are already aware, you just need to *learn*, exactly like you've always done, through people teaching you, or figuring it out for yourself. I can only

80

teach you what I know, the rest you'll have to do the old-fashioned way."

By now I was getting very impatient. "So then, Satan," I said through gritted teeth. "What can you teach me? What do I need to know about these scum, and how am I going to kill them?"

Wickedness filled The Devil's eyes. He motioned for me to take a seat as a chair grew up from the floor beneath me. I sat down as The Devil began to pace back and forth in front of me.

"Let me begin with Gideon," he said.

THREE

"GIDEON," The Devil began, "believes that God has shared with him, and only him, the one secret that could defeat God. What a moron! God I mean, not Gideon. For if Gideon is telling the truth, and I believe he is, then God has gone for one of his mind games again and has left the temptation for Gideon to tell the secret."

"So why don't you tempt him yourself, mighty Satan?" I asked mockingly.

"I can tell by your tone, you know I've tried," he snapped. "Gideon is not tempted by the normal things like women or money, and God has already given him power."

Satan's claws clenched into fists, blood seeping from his palm, where sharp nails had dug through his scaly flesh.

"His first power is to see through my disguises," Satan said as he smeared the blood in his hand over his face. He transformed into a gorgeous woman, with flowing black hair and blood-red lips. His forked tongued flickered out from between them as he smiled and winked. Satan's deep, crooning voice contrasted starkly with his appearance.

"He also has the power of mind control over the weak-willed and so has a small army of disciples at his call who he has named 'The Brethren'. He cannot be harmed by blades or bullets and he has the strength of God in him; no physical barrier will hold him."

"How do I fight someone like that?" I asked. My life as a fighter had taught me a great deal about combat, but my mind couldn't fathom such an adversary.

"Does he have a weakness?" I wondered aloud.

The Devil answered by slashing a claw across his feminine wrist. Black blood gushed from the wound, forming a pool on the carpet at our feet. He licked the gash he'd made, stemming the blood flow as his flesh began to knit itself. I looked down and saw his true face reflected in the ghoulish puddle, grinning up at me. The Devil's facade faded to a vision of Gideon sitting in a room, empty except for a pristine bed that he knelt at in prayer.

My skin crawled watching that evil creature who took so much pleasure in killing my darling Charlotte. Gideon's grating voice filled my ears as he prayed. It felt like daggers being driven into my skull. His head hung against his chest, blonde hair falling over his face. I couldn't see his lips move, only hear the words inside my head, beating at my temples.

"I have done your work my lord," he prayed. "I have done what you asked of me, but forgive me that I enjoyed it. I have sinned and in taking pleasure in this sin I have fouled my soul. I am unclean."

The vision faded back to Satan's reflection grinning up at me again. I looked up to see him rubbing his clawed, black hands together. It was clear he had a plan. However, it was unclear to me what it was. I didn't have to wait long to find out.

"Don't you see?" The Devil asked. "He admits that his soul is tainted, which means if he dies then his soul comes to Hell, to me." His eyes glazed into a fixated stare as he looked down into the pool of his own blood on the ground. Satan began to chant in a strong voice, as if reading a prophecy of biblical proportions.

"You will be re-born to earth, Michael. You will kill Gideon, bringing his soul to Hell where you will have free reign to reap your revenge upon him, and I will be able to discover God's secret. Together, we will overthrow God's power and free all existence from his rule. This is the beginning of Armageddon."

Satan's words were like music to my ears. My mind was fixed on revenge. I could torture Gideon over and over. I could wring Charlotte's suffering from his soul and devour his mind. There would be no secrets left once I had avenged my love.

Purpose filled my every pore and motivation flowed like electricity inside me. Looking over Hell City to the boiling red sky, I knew that one day I would have justice. One day soon I would be reborn. However, unlike most highly motivated people, I had patience. I would prepare to confront Gideon. He had God's power on his side, but I had The Devil.

I turned to Satan, ready to do what I must.

"When do I start my training?" I asked solemnly.

"Right away," he said turning around, walking back toward the elevator.

FOUR

THE DEVIL PRESSED THE GROUND-FLOOR BUTTON. Its red glow lit up his face.

"You must go into the city and find the best path to take in getting back to earth, to defeat Gideon," he said. I could tell by his tone that he would not be coming. I opened my mouth to ask why he would not be joining me, but he cut me off.

"Go to the Prophet Casino in Smoking Gun and seek out a man called Phineus. He will show you the way." The elevator slowed to a halt and the doors slid open. I stepped out, while Satan remained inside. "I will do something else to help you, Michael, because in doing this you are helping me," he said as I turned to look back at him. "I will spare you 'The Guilt'. You won't suffer down here as others do. You are free to do whatever you wish to get what I want. What we want," he corrected himself. "Good luck, Michael. I will see you when you know your path."

Before I could speak, the elevator doors closed, leaving me alone in Hell. I had only one thing on my mind: avenge Charlotte.

I walked across the marbled floor toward the exit. Clytemnestra was not at her desk. A lone doorman stood waiting, with his hands clasped behind his back. He was only four feet high, hideously deformed with green eyebrows that covered most of his face and a hooked nose so long that it touched his wart covered chin.

"Good evening, Michael," he croaked, like a frog. I wasn't surprised he knew my name. "The Dark Lord has provided his limousine for your pleasure. Good luck with Phineus," he laughed.

I turned to him, furious that this little toad of a being knew more than I did about the underworld outside. I hissed through clenched teeth.

"Why should I need luck with The Devil's name at my side?"

He continued to smirk, smug in his knowledge. "Phineus despises Satan."

"Why should he hate Satan?" I fumed.

"Many in Hell do. Some are jealous of his power; some are resentful of being trapped here and blame him instead of God. However, Phineus has a real reason." The toad visibly shook with silent laughter.

"Why?" I asked again.

"The Dark Lord took his eyes," he croaked. "Satan thought they would give him the power to see the future, but stupidly The Devil left his inner eye, the only one that mattered. Phineus hasn't let him close since." The doorman stepped back, opening the doors to the streets of Hell.

"Since you know so much," I said, as I stepped onto the street. "How do I get Phineus to help me?"

"Just pass his test." He slammed the door in my face before I could ask any more questions.

I took a deep breath of scorching air, bringing my raging emotions under control. It would help no-one if I lost my cool. I had to be calculating if I was to help Charlotte. I needed to free her soul as quickly as I could. I couldn't stand the thought that she was in pain, waiting in limbo without me.

Turning towards the street I saw Satan's limousine waiting on the curb, door open. I slid inside. The divider window was already down. The shark-demon driver sat looking at me with black, emotionless eyes.

"I've been told to take you as far as the Prophet Casino," he said in a rasping voice. "After that you're on your own."

He started the car and we lurched out into the traffic. I eased back into my seat, concentrating on my breathing. I didn't want to think of Charlotte or Gideon lest I break down. I needed to be strong and focus on the present, taking each step towards my path of revenge. Right now I needed to find this Phineus.

I looked outside at the sky. It started to burst and bubble and flame. The cars around all swerved and jolted to a halt on the side of the road as the Fires of Guilt rolled over Hell. It was like a black and red inferno all around us. Somehow we kept driving. Looking out on the streets I could make out the shadowy figures of people writhing and contorting on the ground everywhere, consumed by their guilty visions. Black smoke swirled from out of the gutters. It looked like Hell was dying, if that were possible. I was panicking as we surged forward through the firestorm. How was our car still moving in a straight line? I hammered on the tinted glass of the divider-screen and it rolled down to expose the Shark's calm, ugly face. He continued to speed through the bursting maelstrom of fire.

"What are you doing?" I yelled.

"Taking you to the Casino," he answered blankly.

"But why don't you stop because of the visions?" I asked hurriedly.

"Like you, I'm in Satan's employ," he explained as he looked back to the road. "The Devil protects all his employees from the Guilt of God. That's why so many souls work for him. The pay isn't great otherwise."

I leaned back, stunned. I had thought I was the only one, that I was special. It seemed I was wrong. I was just another one of Satan's minions now. It made me feel sick momentarily, but before long thoughts of revenge overwhelmed me again. I could picture Gideon's eyes as he had left me to die. I would soon look into those eyes once more, but he would be the one in pain.

The limo swerved over the curb and I was jolted back to the present. The flames of guilt had subsided and Hell was returning to normal. We drove into the valet parking area in front of a dark purple, glass building. The entire structure was shaped into the form a hooded fortune-teller, hand outstretched onto the footpath holding a crystal ball. Inside the sphere, smoke swirled into various shapes -- mainly items of luxury like cars, boats or piles of gold. Occasionally, I could see myself in there, jumping up and down with fists full of cash, women groping me, pushing others away for a piece of the action. The door of the limo opened by itself, and I stepped back out into the dominating heat of Hell. I was barely out of the car when it squealed away.

I took another deep breath. This was the Prophet Casino, and Phineus was somewhere inside.

FIVE

WALKING INTO THE CASINO, I ignored the other patrons. I had only one purpose here. Anything else was a waste of time.

Inside, it was just like any cliché casino in Vegas: room after room of game tables and poker machines, blinding lights and disorienting carpets. I looked briefly at an old lady slipping coins into a slot machine close to me. It reminded me of my own times of weakness, when I languished in the Riviera Casino rotting my life away. I felt sorry for her. If this was her only pleasure in the world, then she really was in hell. After five minutes of walking along the game floor I was hopelessly lost. I stopped to get my bearings and spotted a bar. Maybe the waitress would know who Phineus was. I sat down on the bar stool, next to a tall African. He wore all black, and his head was shaved to the same length as the stubble on his face. He looked down into his empty drink and swished the ice around, but said nothing.

I motioned to the waitress and she shuffled over to me. She was gorgeous, dressed as a gypsy. Her red blouse was cut in frills around her cleavage, gold necklaces hanging between her breasts, matching the shining metal on her fingers.

"You want a drink," she said, as if declaring the future.

"A vodka and cranberry with lime," I requested.

"Five dollars," she said as she poured the drink. It struck me that I had no money. I hadn't even thought I might have to pay for anything down in Hell, although why not? Money *is* supposed to be the root of all evil. I went to turn my pockets inside out, as if crying poor, but my hand hit a wallet inside. I pulled it from my pants and looked at it. It was stuffed full of hundred dollar bills and credit cards. I had died with it in my pocket.

"Apparently, you *can* take it with you," I said handing over a crisp green note, but she didn't get the joke. "My friend here will have another as well." I nodded my head toward the African next to me and he looked up.

"Thank you," he said, smiling genuinely, his white teeth splitting the darkness of his face. "You're new to Hell?" he asked.

"I am. Is it that obvious?" I replied, taking a sip of my vodka as he picked up his bubbling concoction from the bar.

"Most people here wouldn't dare to talk to a stranger. Everyone is scared of becoming the prey of demons."

"I've been told that this is a place of rehabilitation," I replied.

The African grunted into his drink. "It is for some. I have seen many souls pass over to Heaven, many who realize the errors of their ways. It's funny, though, the strong are the ones who survive best down here. They do what they please, and make full use of the opportunity to actually enjoy Damnation. However, it's those strong predators that eventually turn to demons and get stuck down here for all of eternity, in the heat and the stink of Hell. It's the weak who really succeed. The ones who suffer are the ones who learn the most about themselves and why they are here. The preyed upon are the ones who eventually move on. The losers win and the winners lose. Hell is a strange place."

He paused and took a sip of his drink. I nodded along, pretending I knew what the stranger was talking about.

"Say, do you know a guy called Phineus?" I asked, going for the direct approach.

"No," he said. "Should I?"

"I don't know," I shrugged. "I guess not. I'm Michael." I held out my hand and he took it in a strong grip.

"Marlowe," he said shaking my hand. "Welcome to Hell, Michael. You'll like it here. You look like one of the strong ones."

"I don't plan on staying too long," I said in answer. He almost choked on his drink, but recovered quickly.

"Well, you're in the right place to start purging those sins, Michael. You'll just need a lot of money to do it."

As Marlowe finished his sentence, an old man crashed into the roulette table closest to the bar. Two muscle-laden bouncers lunged in and dragged him to his feet, pummeling him with punches to the face and stomach. I jumped to my feet and Marlowe grabbed my arm.

"This isn't your fight, Michael," he said, but I wasn't listening.

"He's blind!" was all I replied in explanation. I shook free of his grip and followed the bouncers as they dragged the blind man through the casino by his heels, making sure his head whacked every table leg on the way past. As they got close to the door, they picked up his now limp body and tossed him out onto the sidewalk. He rolled head first into the tire of a parked car and stopped.

"Don't come back, cheater," one of the apes spat and they walked back inside, leaving the elderly man unconscious on the ground.

I ran to his side and rolled him over. He had a blindfold wrapped over his face, which had two circular patches of blood where his eyes would have been. I slapped him lightly on the cheek, trying to rouse him.

"Phineus, Phineus," I said in a loud voice.

"How do you know my name, Michael?" he groaned as he sat up rubbing his temples.

SIX

"HOW DO YOU KNOW *my* name is a more appropriate question at this stage," I said, exasperated at how in hell Phineus could know who I was.

"I know many things," he answered cryptically as he leant forward, resting his elbows on his knees for support. "I know your name is Michael, and I know why you are here to find me. What I don't know is who sent you and how you know my name, but that is because I cannot seem to see the answer."

"The Devil sent me," I replied, believing honesty was the best policy here. "He told me your name. Another told me I was looking for a man with no eyes. I have come seeking answers."

"You think you have come seeking answers," he said. "But if Satan sent you, then what you *think* you are here for and why you *are* indeed here is not the same thing. However, let's assume you know why you seek me."

I could already tell that getting answers out of this riddler wouldn't be easy. I could barely grasp what he was saying, and we hadn't even talked for a few minutes.

"Let's at least go somewhere private," I said, helping him to his feet. "We can talk about what it is I think I want to know from you."

"At least you're a quick learner," he laughed. "Very smart for someone who usually uses his fists instead of his brain. Follow me and we'll talk some more."

Phineus seemed to shake off his beating with little more than a shrug. He grabbed my arm, pulling me towards the road. I was being led across a busy highway by a blind man. Cars were swerving and honking their horns at us. Phineus hobbled unwavering through the traffic, directly across the road to a small shack of a building which was wedged between two phallic brothels. The building, made completely of rotting wood, looked like it would collapse at any second. The broken windows were caked with mud and cobwebs, so you couldn't see through them. Phineus pulled out a key and unlocked the front door, beckoning me to enter. Within was a complete contrast to what I saw on the outside of the building. It was clean, luxurious and cool.

Phineus led me inside. The interior was painted all white, almost like this was a glowing replica of Heaven. A white rug covered white tile floors. He motioned for me to sit on a white leather couch which had tall black hourglasses sitting at each end like two symbolic bookends.

I looked around the apartment. There were all the creature comforts of a modern home. A sunken lounge room to the right had a ridiculously large plasma TV hanging on the wall. Surround-sound speakers were placed everywhere. Up three steps on the other side of the room was another entertaining area with a pool table, dartboard and a fully stocked bar. Leading on from the bar was a long hallway which went through to where the master bedroom should be. However, this portion of the house wasn't lit so I could see no further.

"This is not what I expected from the outside!" I blurted.

"Appearances can be deceiving; you would do well to remember that," Phineus said. "Leaving the outside as it is works much better than any security system against would-be thieves. Why bother breaking in somewhere that has nothing to offer?" Phineus slowly lowered himself onto the ground. His knees cracked as he pulled his legs into a cross-legged position on a rug in front of the couch. He rested his hands on his thighs in the meditation position. I sat and waited in silence for him to speak again. He seemed deep in thought, as if staring into space with his blood-patch eyes.

"You are here for love," he spoke finally. "You are here for yourself, not that Devil. For this I am glad, otherwise I would not help you, for he is the origin of all lies."

I sat still and silent not willing to interrupt his concentration.

"I know the path you must take to fulfill your true destiny; it is a path full of deceit. I can guide you. Tell you the most efficient way to succeed in your revenge. Without me, your quest would take years. Instead it will take only weeks. But..." he stopped and stood, turning his back on me.

"But, what?" I asked after him. "I will do whatever you want of me."

"You would," he said. "I can see this. The question is *can* you? I do not require you to pass a test of the physical realm, but of the mental. Logic must be combined with your strength of body and determination of spirit if you are to succeed in your task. You must demonstrate to me your capacity for thought and logic under pressure, regardless of how illogical or impossible the challenge may seem."

I sat, ready for anything, ready to hurl myself into any life-threatening situation Phineus might thrust upon me. I would do anything to help Charlotte.

"You must answer my riddle," he said.

I almost burst out laughing.

"Is that all?" I scoffed. "What is this riddle? I will figure it out with time."

"Will you?" he sounded doubtful. "You realize that only a handful of souls have ever passed my test. Some of the greatest minds in history have not cracked my puzzle, and if you don't succeed you will leave here and I will never, ever help you." He paused, waiting for what he'd just said to sink in, then continued.

"This is my riddle:
The person who makes me does not need me
The person who buys me does not want me or use me and

94

The person who uses me does not know that they are using me."

I closed my eyes and began to think; this might take weeks to figure out, but I had all the time in hell.

"You have one hour to give me an answer," Phineus said, turning one of the sand-filled hourglasses near the couch on its hinges.

SEVEN

I ROSE FROM PHINEUS' COUCH IN ANGER.

"What?" I snapped. "You never said anything about a time limit."

"I just did," Phineus replied in annoyance. "This is a test, not a homework assignment that you can take home and look up the answers on Google. What do you think this is? Play time, maybe?" His eyebrows arched with his question. As they came back down, the bandage covering his eyes fell around his neck. It was a ghastly sight, still bleeding sockets dripping congealed blood. They were empty, red voids with veins and nerve endings still writhing around inside, like little black and blue worms searching for light. I gasped and fell back onto the couch.

"How long ago did Satan take your eyes?" I whispered in horror.

"Over two thousand years ago," Phineus replied as he pulled the blindfold back up over his deformity.

"Surely they would have healed by now?" I asked.

"Nothing dies in Hell, Michael, since we are already dead," he said. "My eyes are still alive somewhere in that Devil's castle, waiting to be returned to their rightful owner. If I ever get them back, they will knit and mend and I will be whole again. But I gave up hope of this long ago. I dare not go near Satan lest he take what he really wanted in the first place, my inner eye, which is much more important to me than static sight."

"Does it still hurt?" I ventured.

"As much today as the morning he ripped them from my face with his pointed claws. This is Hell, Michael. You would be a fool to think that it is not a place of suffering. Enough chitchat now, man. You've already wasted valuable time. You now have fifty minutes. Be back before then with an answer, or I will not help you."

96

He motioned toward the hourglass with his hand as if to emphasize his point. The black grains tumbled through the narrow middle and into the bulbous lower end, forming a neat pyramid of sand in the glass cage. The physical effect of watching my time drain away had more impact than any ticking clock. My mind went blank.

Phineus ushered me from his pristine lounge and pushed me out of the door, closing it quietly behind me. I stumbled onto the street of Smoking Gun, my head a jumbled mess of questions. I felt like I had cotton balls stuffed in my ears. Noise from the world around me was muffled by the sound of my own thoughts. Sweat began pouring down my face. The hellish heat clamped around me, making it even harder to think clearly. I needed to concentrate. *Why would you buy something if you don't want it? Why would you make something you don't need?* These were ridiculous questions. Phineus was resting my hope of revenge on a child's game, but he was serious so I had to be as well.

I was no novice at solving puzzles. When I was younger, the nuns at my orphanage would test us with riddles to keep us occupied and keep our minds sharp. I would walk around the school grounds for hours at a time, forever turning these problems over in my head until I came up with the correct answer. Somehow walking always helped me think, so that's what I did. I began to walk down the footpath, past garish casinos and rundown watering holes, through the suburb of Smoking Gun. The streets were busy. Demons and humans walked by, paying no attention to me as I muttered possible answers to myself. No matter how much I thought, no answer came. A condom maybe? The contraceptive pill? Possibly poison? One thing about riddles is that when you get the answer, you know it's correct without doubt before you confirm it with the riddler. I was running out of time, and fast. I'd already been walking aimlessly around in the stifling heat for half an hour. I could never get a riddle this fast as a kid, and that wasn't changing now.

I rounded the block so I could keep close to Phineus' house, in case the answer came to me. Now in a quieter strip of shops, there was barely any sound, just the low hum of traffic and the distant beat of a drum. I stopped and listened. It seemed to be coming closer and closer, like a creeping heartbeat. As the drum pounded louder I could hear a mass of footsteps, stomping in time. There were voices as well. Where was it coming from? At that moment, a cavalcade of demons and half-demons, dressed in vibrant colors, pranced out from a side alleyway in front of me, into the middle of the road. They were chanting and singing wildly in a language I couldn't understand, cheering at regular intervals. One demon, dressed all in black with a red top hat, spat fire from his mouth into the air. I stood back as the parade marched past. There were massive skulls bobbing on floats, and skeletons hanging from poles that the revelers held high over their own ghastly heads.

The procession snaked down the road and then veered off down another lane, like a demented Mardi Gras, celebrating death. It was very similar to something I saw once in Mexico, called Dia De Los Muertos -- the Day of the Dead. It was a day where passed loved ones were remembered in celebration, rather than mourning.

I snapped out of my lapse in concentration, shutting out the noise and confusing colors of the parade. I had to concentrate on the task at hand. I had to think, and fast.

The secret of solving a riddle is finding the most illogical part of the problem and making it logical under a special circumstance. It seemed that the last part of this puzzle held the key to the solution.

"How could I be using something and not know I am actually using it?" I asked aloud. Then it hit me like punch in the face. How could I not have seen it right away? I looked at my watch, three minutes left. I sprinted back towards Phineus' home. I knew the answer to his little test, but I was out of time!

EIGHT

"A COFFIN!" I yelled in triumph as I burst through Phineus' door, seconds before the final grains of sand slid to rest in the hour glass at his side. He smiled without looking up.

"Very good, Michael. You're the first person for around a thousand years to have answered correctly in time. Of course, I knew you would," he said. "I saw it."

"You know how strange that sounds coming from a blind man," I said cheekily.

"Oh, we are happy with ourself, are we?" he taunted back. "That was one silly riddle. The rest of your journey will prove a lot tougher, and you only just pulled this one off in the nick of time. In the future you'll need to be much faster on your toes, quick of body and of mind to gain your revenge on Gideon."

"You have already seen what I must do?" I asked excitedly, grabbing him by the shoulders and shaking him, as if I was trying to rattle the answer from his mouth.

"Indeed, Michael, but you must have patience," he said. "You must steady yourself and be focused. Now take a seat, I'll show you what you must do and where you must go to destroy your hatred. You realize that this is not the *only* path you can take and it is surely not the easiest, but it is the best. I must warn you now that this is only what you *think* you want to achieve, but nothing I can say will make your purpose any different. Remember that freewill plays a part in everything you do. No-one's destiny is set in concrete. This is the most probable outcome of the path, but not the only one. I am not here to tell you how it will be, but how it may be. You must do the rest."

"I understand," I lied, sinking into the couch. "I am ready to do what I must."

Phineus sat cross-legged on the ground again at my feet and reached out, searching for my hands. I grabbed his fingers, and he clasped his palms over my fists. His touch instantly made me nauseous. Pulsating shocks ran from his hands through my body, zapping up into my forehead. The world around caved in on itself and revealed flashing visions, bursting through my mind like a strobe.

I saw a pitch black alleyway with a faintly lit door, flaked, yellow paint peeling off it. A shadowy figure was blocking the way. Flash. A creature, human-like, bald, covered in eyes, one of them open. I fell inside one of the eyes, through a ball of flame and a rush of water. Flash. An Egyptian laughing at me, his face painted blue, a black and gold Falcon flapping its wings on his head. He cut my wrists and wrung the blood into a bowl. Flash. The Egyptian's face turned into Gideon swinging a sword of fire toward my face. Then all went blank.

I sat up gasping for air. It felt like I'd been underwater. My ears were ringing. The room around me was dark. It felt like it was night time outside, if there was such a thing in Hell.

I thought I'd only been out for minutes, but hours must have gone by. There was no sound from the street outside, no traffic, nothing. Phineus was nowhere to be seen. I called out his name but there was no answer. After a full minute I rose slowly, aching all over. I limped painfully to the kitchen where I turned on the tap and splashed some water on my face, clearing my buzzing head. Finally, the ringing stopped and I flicked on the light switch.

Blood splatters covered the walls and floor. Somehow, I knew it was the blood of Phineus. There was a pool of it at the foot of the couch where he had been sitting and then a trail, like he'd been dragged over the floor and out into the street. I frantically ran to the door; there was a note stuck to it. It read:

Find the Perceptionist with a thousand eyes
Down the yellow-door lane in Satan's Demise
Take a gift of gold as a gift of thread
And the eyes that belong in Phineus' head
There you will learn the power of sight
To create to destroy is Michael's birthright
The Elemental's secret will soon be revealed
And Michael's dark fate forever is sealed.

I read the note over and over again. Most of it didn't make sense. There was only one person who could help me from here: Satan.

NINE

I LOCKED THE DOOR BEHIND ME as I left Phineus' home. I hoped that he was okay, but I had a more urgent matter at hand -- revenge. I wasn't certain how I would find Satan, but surely it wouldn't be too hard to find the Dark Lord of Hell in his own domain. I thought about going back to his building. As I looked to the skyline of Hell, I saw the tip of the mountain where he had told me his home was. Casa Diablo. That's exactly where he would be. I felt it.

I stuck my arm in the air, hailing one of the blood-red taxis that were whizzing past. The closest car slammed on its breaks and squealed up to the curb. A burly cab-driver with a tattoo of a naked lady on his arm leant out of his window and snarled, "You better have some freaking money, buddy."

I pulled a hundred dollar bill out of my pocket and waved it in his face. Suddenly smiling, he chirped, "Jump in the front, someone just threw up back there and I haven't cleaned it up yet."

I walked around the side of the car and climbed into the passenger seat.

"Take me to Casa Diablo," I said.

He shook his head in dismay. "Have you lost your mind there, buddy?" he said in a thick, New Jersey accent. "This cab don't fly, you can't get up there without a chopper."

"Then take me to a chopper," I said abruptly.

"Whoa, alright then, chief, I know just the crazy bastard for the job," he said, slamming his foot to the floor and boosting out onto the highway.

The stench of vomit from the back seat consumed the entire cab, making me feel ill. It smelt like bin-juice and alcohol mixed together. The driver swerved and dodged through traffic making matters worse. I swallowed the bile rising in my throat.

"You sure this cab can't fly?" I joked, trying to keep my mind off the smell. "Sure feels like we could take off at any moment."

"Say, you're alright," he laughed. "The name's Mack. I've been driving cabs half my life, and all of my death." He grinned at me, a few teeth missing from his smile. "I'm glad you had some cash, I've been driving around that place all day and everyone I go to pick up wants a lift for free, 'cos they've lost all their bread in the casinos."

"Yeah, well I don't gamble," I said seriously.

"I guess there's more to do in Smoking Gun than flush yer bread down the toilet." He winked.

"I guess so," I replied. "Where are we headed anyway?" The putrid reek of sick in the backseat was making me feel queasy again. I needed to get out of this cab. It felt like the smell was suffocating me.

"Smithy's Hanger," Mack replied. "He's a freakin' nut if you ask me, but that's what you'll need if you want someone to fly you up to that peak. Most air-traffic up there gets crushed by Satan's pet dragon, Moloch, like little flies between the fingers of wanton boys." He pinched his thumb and forefinger together and made a squishing noise to emphasize his point.

"How long have we got to go?" I asked as buildings and cars sped by. "I think I'm about to add to the mess there in the back if we don't pull over soon."

The words barely escaped my mouth when Mack pulled on his handbrake. We slid sideways, screeching into a gravel driveway just off the main road. The car fishtailed, but he regained control and accelerated toward a seemingly abandoned aircraft hangar.

There was rust showing through the corrugated iron cladding of the domed structure. The grounds around it were littered with old World War I and II bi-planes, Spitfires, F-16 fighter jets and Blackhawk helicopters. It reminded me of an aircraft graveyard. Mack slid to a stop next to a dilapidated office and I fell out of the passenger door, retching fluro-yellow stomach lining onto the ground. Fresh air filled my lungs and I began to breath normally again. I wiped the spittle from my chin and stumbled to my feet, glad to be out of the putrid taxi.

"Here you are, buddy," Mack said, slapping me on the shoulders, "Kingsford Aviation. The owner, Smithy is a good friend of mine. He's an old war hero or something, although he doesn't like to bring it up. I can help you talk him into flying up to that mountain, for a nice little tip of course," he said winking.

"Get me a good price and I'll give you another one of these," I said, clapping a hundred-dollar bill into his palm.

"Righto, buddy," he beamed. "I'll get a price The Devil would be proud of."

I followed Mack into the office, through an open sliding-glass door. Inside looked more like a war museum than a charter service. Old flags lined the walls, and pictures of vintage aircraft and war medals hung in frames behind the desk, where an old pilot sat. His face was shriveled up and wrinkly like a crusty sultana. A worn leather flying cap and goggles were pulled firm over his head. White, curly hair protruded from underneath the earflaps on either side. His mouth hung open and his snores filled the room. Drool dribbled from the corner of his mouth, plopping to the ground at the base of his stool and forming a puddle on the floor.

Mack slapped his meaty hand on the counter and shouted, "Air raid!" at the top of his lungs.

The senior citizen before us sprang into action, jumping to his feet and leaping the counter with surprising agility. He ran right past us and out the open door towards his hangar, gazing up at the sky for incoming planes. His run slowed to a jog when he failed to see anything threatening flying overhead. Eventually, he stopped, eyes glued to the black clouds above.

"Smithy, you old idiot!" Mack yelled out the door, waving his hand in greeting. "You fall for that air raid shit every bloody time." He looked at me laughing. "Every time!" he said again, shaking his head in disbelief.

Smithy slowly walked back to the front of the office where we were now standing, wagging his finger in the air at Mack.

"Mack, you scoundrel! How many times do I have to tell you a soldier can never give up his training? I'm always ready for some new action."

He finally made it to where we were standing and embraced Mack with a hug of true friends. I could tell the luck of the devil was running at my side. I put my hand out and introduced myself.

"Hello Smithy, I'm Michael, I'm..." Mack cut me off.

"We've got a dangerous assignment for you, soldier," Mack said theatrically. "Only a pilot of your immense skill and daring could possibly pull it off."

Smithy's chest swelled with pride as Mack continued.

"This is a perilous mission now, Smithy. We'll need only the best craft in your fleet to undertake the task, your AH-64 Apache."

The pilot's smile turned to a frown. "Mack, I hope you don't want me to fly up to that castle again?" he said flatly.

My hopes dimmed.

"But of course," Mack continued, not missing a beat. "Only the best of the best can make it past Moloch to the safety of Casa Diablo, on the peak of Mount Belial. You are the only person who could pull such a feat off, don't you agree?" he baited.

"I guess you are right there," Smithy conceded. "But it will cost an awful lot for such a dangerous mission."

My heart sank even further; I only had a few hundred dollars left in my pocket.

"Name your price!" Mack said confidently.

Smithy rubbed his chin as if deep in thought.

"Well, I would say it would cost you around fifty dollars plus twenty five for fuel!" he said, as if asking an outrageous amount.

Mack whispered out the side of this mouth, "He still thinks it's 1945."

"Deal!" Mack said to Smithy. "We are willing to pay the best for the best."

I pulled out three hundred dollars from the wad in my pocket. I gave a hundred to Mack and two hundred to Smithy.

"You can keep the change if you wait for me and bring me back safely," I said.

His eyes almost popped out of his head looking at the money I gave him, then he looked back up at me.

"You government?" he asked. "Only government could afford such a price."

Mack stamped on my foot, indicating to play along.

"Yes I am," I said solemnly. "I'm on a top-secret assignment of espionage on The Devil himself." I leant in, lowering my voice to a whisper. "You must realize I'm paying for your silence as well as your services."

"Why, of course," he replied now whispering also. "You can be assured I'll not tell a word of your trip to any demon, no matter how fierce. Those creatures need to be brought down by someone!" He snapped his hand to his forehead in salute and began to march toward his hangar.

"Follow me, captain," he shouted back. "We leave immediately."

TEN

I FOLLOWED SMITHY TOWARD THE HANGAR, yelling at Mack, "Catch you later. I'll need a lift when we return if you're around."

"I'll make sure I am," he shouted back. I turned and jogged to catch up to my geriatric pilot, who was just entering his rusted hanger. I stopped dead as I entered. In the centre of the building was a crisp shining chopper, painted to resemble a tiger. Black and yellow stripes glistened under the halogen globes attached to the ceiling. The sharp rotors hung limp, ready to twist into action. Smithy was about four feet away, pulling on a khaki jump suit and black, lace-up boots. He looked up, steely eyed and smiling from ear to ear. He pulled his goggles down over his eyes and snapped his ear-flaps into place under his chin. He threw me a jump suit.

"Put that on before we board, Captain," he said. "You're in for a hell of a ride. We'll be encountering one mischievous bogie on this flight. Le Dragon Rouge, Moloch the Great; he's destroyed more choppers and planes than the Japanese and Germans combined."

I pulled on my suit and followed Smithy's lead as he climbed into the pilot's chair, me in the jump seat.

"Prepare for takeoff," Smithy said as he flicked switches on his dash and clipped his seatbelt over his shoulder. "We'll have to leave right away if we are to get up there before the next wave of Guilt sweeps us all into oblivion."

It was hard to believe this quirky man could be guilty of anything worthy of keeping him in Hell, but I knew better than to ask that sort of personal question. Smithy pushed a remote control button to his left. The roof of the hangar slowly slid open, bathing us in Hell's bloody glow. The rotors of the

107

chopper whirred into life and picked up speed. The sound of steel blades slicing the air filled my ears. Smithy eased the joystick back between his legs and we rose into the air, slowly at first, then faster, moving upwards and outwards, soaring above Hell City.

The spider web of streets stretched out below us as we flew above the skyscrapers and casinos. I looked up to the mountain and saw lights glowing in The Devil's castle. Someone was home.

Smithy's voice crackled through the headphones I had on. "Great view, isn't it!" he said. "Such a beautiful angle of a horrible place."

I nodded agreement and pointed to where the city went dark, just beyond the dazzling lights of Smoking Gun.

"Why don't the lights work in that part of town?" I asked through my mic.

"That's the suburb of Satan's Demise," he said. "It's the heart of darkness, a place of powerful demons that often come out and attack Satan, or the other parts of Hell, for no apparent reason. No-one will ever go there to service the city's lights or buildings, so it grows forever darker. It's a place you'd never want to visit if you can help it."

"Satan's Demise," I repeated, alarm bells going off in my head. I pulled the piece of paper out of my pocket; *Find the Perceptionist with a thousand eyes / Down the yellow-door lane in Satan's Demise.* It seemed I would be going to that most evil part of Hell before too long.

Smithy pointed ahead as Mount Belial loomed in front of us. It was ugly, black and dominating. As we got closer I could see the twisted trees that covered the mountainside. They looked like people frozen in agony. Anguished faces pushed out from the trunks. Branches reached for the sky, like outstretched arms with broken twigs for fingers.

"They almost look alive," I gasped.

"They are," Smithy said with a melancholy look on his face. "Those are the lost souls who took their own lives on earth. Suicide is punished for ten thousand years on the mountain. Apparently, God doesn't like the gift of life being thrown back in his face."

I looked back down at the trees. Never before had I seen such sorrow on faces etched in the woods below. They were suffering in pain absolute. Ravens hung in their branches and cawed up at us, warning us away from the forest. Most of the birds were perched at the side of the trees, constantly wailing croaky cries. It sounded like they were saying 'forever more, forever more'. Suddenly, every one of the black ravens launched from its perch and flew away screeching, as if startled. Smithy's voice crackled once again in my ears.

"You'd better hold on tight, Captain," he cried, pulling back hard on the controls. A whoosh of red, flapping wings and scales streaked past to the right of us as we shot straight up into the air. My heart leapt into my throat. Satan's dragon was upon us.

Above the thump, thump of the chopper's blades I heard a mighty roar. I looked up to behold a crimson lizard, covered in armored scales. Its snout was short and fat, crisscrossed in scars and wrinkles. Its horns jutted out the top of his head, in a twisted row of spikes that continued down his back and all the way to his tail. Smoke seeped out of his nostrils and yellow, incisor-teeth poked up from under his gums. He spread his gigantic wings wide, like a huge vampire bat. The monster gnashed his teeth and screeched another roar of terror. This was Moloch.

He turned midair, bloody wings propelling him toward our aircraft, which looked like a floating bumblebee compared with this red-scaled albatross. I turned to see the beast advancing, gaining ground rapidly. Jets of fire spurted from his nostrils as he approached. The torrent of flame barely missed our tail. He roared again showing razor teeth, each one a jagged, yellow sword ready to cleave open our chopper like a tin can. Smithy pushed down on the joystick and we dove forward, Moloch's jaws snapping above us. They chomped down on empty air as we lurched into a death-dive straight toward the mountainside.

Skeletons of other choppers and planes lay scattered amongst the trees below, like trophies of the terrible lizard behind us. The ground rushed up at us at top speed, Moloch roaring in attack behind us, closing ground fast as we sped towards certain destruction against the black mountain. Smithy giggled like a school boy and wrenched the joystick of the chopper forward again, executing a reverse pull up. The blades of the chopper faced the ground as we looped underneath the mighty dragon.

Moloch whipped his barbed tail at us as we sped back up into the air. It clipped our rear rotor, sending us into a spin. The dragon screamed again, but this time in pain as the blade of the rotor sliced a thick chunk of meat out of his tail. Smithy shakily brought the Apache under control. I could hear a clunking noise coming from the rear.

"The blade back there is bent!" I yelled at Smithy, looking behind at the damage the dragon's tail had caused.

"I know!" he cried, "That's our stabilizing rotator. I've lost fifty percent control of the chopper. We're in for a rough ride!"

I looked down at our attacker as the chopper lurched and rattled in the air. Moloch was now sitting crouched on the mountainside looking up at us with intelligent eyes, his tail leaking green blood onto the ground around him. His eyes narrowed. It looked as though he'd seen our weakness and was getting ready to pounce, appearing now more like a lion than a lizard.

The Dragon pushed hard off the ground with his thick legs, and propelled himself straight up at us, wings tucked in tight at his sides allowing for maximum speed. Smithy leaned on the controls once more and we dove down to meet the red beast. Smithy flipped a switch on his dash and pushed a glowing, red button. With a hiss, two missiles shot from our undercarriage straight into Moloch's roaring mouth. He closed his jaws and pulled short his attack, flapping in mid-air, startled. A look of bewilderment briefly showed on his face before he swallowed loudly. I heard a faint rumble as the missiles detonated inside him. The dragon let out a reeking burp and black smoke wisped out of his mouth and nostrils. Moloch bellowed a furious snarl.

"Those missiles had nuclear heads on them!" Smithy gasped in astonishment.

"I guess his insides are used to fire!" I shot back. We both sat in the chopper, gaping at the beast in front of us as he regained his composure, readying himself for another attack. He swooped around us in large loops, looking for the best way to dive in, like a circling shark.

"I've got a plan," Smithy said, and wheeled the chopper around shakily, steadying the tail before darting right at the dragon.

"What the hell are you doing?" I yelled. "You're going to kill us!"

Our brazen attack took Moloch by surprise and he backed up in the air, flaring his wings as he did. Smithy took his shot and fired the guns of the chopper. Searing lead blasted out of our artillery and sliced through the thin flesh that made up the bulk of the dragon's wingspan. Moloch shrieked in agony and curled into a ball, tumbling toward the ground. He crashed down with a horrific thud into the forest of the damned below, and lay still on the mountainside.

"He's not dead," Smithy said, disappointed, as he motioned toward the dragon below. It struggled to its feet before falling back down and breathing heavily. Moloch was bleeding from his wings now, as well as his tail.

"Dragons recover very quickly," he said. "We'd better get to Casa Diablo before he comes back angrier than ever."

111

Smithy straightened the chopper and made a bee-line for the peak. We hobbled in our crippled bird toward the tip of the mountain. Satan's palace soon came into view.

ELEVEN

CASA DIABLO WAS BRIGHTLY LIT. It was a mix between an old English castle and a modern day resort. Towering Gothic spires loomed above tennis courts and swimming pools. Green gardens flourished around a great hedge labyrinth to the west of the castle, while a huge steaming lake bubbled to the east side of the grounds. We circled above in the chopper, and Smithy spotted a large helipad, painted white and red below in the centre of the main courtyard. He took the bird down, gently floating to land as a dark, horned figure strode out to greet us. We waited for the blades to slow to a halt before exiting the aircraft. A ghastly demon dressed in a tuxedo bowed in greeting before us.

"Hello, Sir Michael," he said. "The Dark Master has told me of your arrival."

The demon's horns wound out of his head and inwards like a ram. They had black lines circling around them at half-inch intervals. A tuft of black hair grew out of his skull between them, contrasting with his bright-red skin. His orange eyes had three, tiny dots of black in the centre where his pupils should have been, and he had no eyelids that I could see. It made him look almost feline.

"I am Azazel, his Lordship's servant. Please follow me." He said, turning on his heels as he strode away from the chopper, back over a large lush lawn toward the castle proper.

We followed Azazel across the lawn and climbed a wide set of grey steps toward the main entrance. It had hideous gargoyles perched at either side of two carved, oak doors. One of the gargoyles looked a lot like Moloch, but more disfigured with boar-like tusks sticking out either side of its mouth, and a long, wispy goatee hanging down over sharp claws. The statue opened its stone eyes and looked at me, growling in its throat. I jumped a full step backwards in surprise. Its eyes snapped shut again before I could be sure I'd even seen them open in the first place. Swallowing my surprise, I followed Azazel inside as he pushed open one of the oak doors. Smithy was close on my heels, looking back in fright at the two stone sentinels beside the front door.

The interior of the mansion was extremely luxurious, carpeted with thick Persian rugs and macabre paintings lining the walls. One work by William Blake featured prominently. It was a watercolor near my shoulder, set in what looked like a solid diamond frame. The painting depicted a white, muscular figure with three heads looking up to another fiery, winged creature in front of it. Below the painting was inscribed: The Number of The Beast is 666.

"It's the original!" a voice boomed from above. "I posed for that back in the day. It's amazing what William came up with, from me sitting alone in a bare room, dressed in a suit!"

I looked up to see The Devil striding down the stairs holding his arms wide in greeting. "Welcome to my humble home, Michael. I've been waiting for you! I trust all went well with Phineus?"

"In a manner of speaking," I said. "All I really got were some obscure visions and a riddle, but it's a start."

"You must tell me all about it right away," he said. "I see you've brought the famous Smithy with you!"

"How do you know my pilot?" I asked.

"Come now," Satan said reproachfully. "I know every creature that resides in Hell, but Smithy holds a special place for me. I rescued this old soul from the forest of the doomed, where he lay in torment for taking his own life. I took pity on his suffering and in return he used to fly me back and forth up to my home."

I looked at Smithy, who was staring at Satan with hate in his eyes. He then looked to me sadly. "He tells the truth, Michael. I did take my own life. I couldn't stand the pain of having killed innocent people during the war. I'm still haunted by their faces. I was weak but I make no excuses, I deserve to be damned."

"There you go again, Smithy," The Devil chuckled next to me. "You were under orders. You killed those people under duress. There is no fault with that. But you cannot forgive *yourself*, which is why you're trapped here. That is your sin, Smithy."

"No it isn't," Smithy growled at him and then turned back to me. "He lies, Michael, don't listen to his deceit or he'll own you. I have done wrong and now I must repent for my murders in Damnation forever. That's why he wouldn't employ me anymore, isn't that right, Satan? Because I refused to be spared The Guilt."

"Well, what use is a pilot if you can't fly at any time, Smithy?" Satan smiled at him. "I need to go places, even when the souls of Hell are tormented by their visions. I'm much more satisfied with my lovely pet dragon, who I hear you tussled with on the way up here. He's licking his wounds down in the caves beneath us. Don't worry, he'll be back on his feet in no time. I've told him to leave you alone on your return."

For some reason I didn't feel reassured. Smithy recoiled from Satan and hid behind me, as if I could protect him from The Devil's penetrating glare.

"It's okay, Old Timer," The Devil taunted. "I'm not mad at you. You've brought my friend here back to me when I need him most. Azazel will make sure you're comfortable while we're gone. You can have your precious visions of Guilt in peace. Michael and I have much to discuss. I'll even ensure any damage done to your Apache is fixed while you're here, to show my appreciation."

The Devil clicked his fingers and his servant stepped forward, taking Smithy by the arm and leading him out of the room. He began to protest, but I placated him.

"It's okay. I'll be back before you know it. I've got his trust now. I should be able to get to him sooner than I thought! Keep your eyes open for anything suspicious," I whispered.

"I'll report any extra intelligence to you on the flight back, Mr. Double Agent," he winked, a toothy grin returning to his wrinkled face.

I turned back to Satan. "Where do I begin?" I asked.

"Begin with your visions from Phineus," he said.

I recounted what I saw in my visions triggered by the blind man. The alley with the yellow door, the thousand-eyed demon, fire, water, the Egyptian and finally Gideon swinging his fiery sword.

"And then there is this," I said, handing over the riddle from Phineus' door.

He read it aloud.

"Find the Perceptionist with a thousand eyes / Down the yellow-door lane in Satan's Demise / Take a gift of gold as a gift of thread / And the eyes that belong in Phineus' head / There you will learn the power of sight / To create to destroy is Michael's birthright / The Elemental's secret will soon be revealed / And Michael's dark fate forever is sealed."

Satan growled with rage and the paper in his hands burst into a green flame. It burnt brightly for a second before turning to black ash, which he blew from his hand. He turned his back on me and strode around the room, muttering to himself. After six laps of the room he stopped and smiled at me.

"Let's go get a drink," he said. "It's time I told you a few things."

TWELVE

I FOLLOWED SATAN UP THE STAIRWAY to the second floor of his mansion. We walked through twisting corridors lined with the artwork of painters such as Salvador Dali, Da Vinci and Michelangelo. There were many others who I'd never heard of. I even saw a cityscape of Howard Arkley's that I had loved when I was alive. The paintings ranged from the surreal to deeply religious. All were absolute works of genius.

"I love art," The Devil said as he saw me admiring the paintings on the wall. "The scientists up on Earth have it all wrong. All they do is try to explain life by answering meaningless questions. The artists, they *give* meaning, they're the ones who make life worth living." I was surprised at the side of Satan I was seeing, much more like a philosopher than some dark overlord.

He continued in silence and finally came to a large open library, filled with rows and rows of books, stuffed in shelves in seemingly random order. He motioned for me to sit down on one of two chairs which were placed in a cleared area amongst the piles of text. I took a seat, looking at a decanter of deep amber fluid on a coffee table between the chairs. The Devil saw me looking at it and poured me a glass. I smelled the contents. The unmistakable aroma of malt whiskey teased my senses.

"Only the best, Michael, only the best," The Devil said as he sat down in the seat opposite me.

My chair was extremely comfortable, covered in soft, suede-leather and loosely stuffed so I sunk back into its deep seat and high back. Satan leaned back into his own chair, folding his claws and placing them on top of his crossed legs like an old English dandy.

He let out a large sigh.

"Oh, where to begin?" he asked aloud to no one in particular. "There is so much to tell, we could be stuck here all millennia. I think I'll start with the important stuff; the rest is really quite trivial when you get down to it."

He let out another sigh and leaned further back into his chair, clicking his tongue and looking up into the air, as if pondering the best way to start his story. He then looked me right in the eyes and began.

"The fundamental problem with all questions about how life started is this: at some point, there has to be something that just *was*. It was there from nothing." He paused and waited for me to wrap my mind around the thought.

"In the beginning," he continued, "there was a single consciousness. I guess you could call it God. This God came into being by *realizing* he existed, spawning himself from his own consciousness. He willed himself into life. By drawing from around him the elements at hand, he manifested a physical form, his body. This is why you will sometimes hear God referred to as The Elemental, because He made himself from the things in nothingness that were somehow just 'there' to begin with. Not even God can tell you how the elements got there."

I drained the contents of my glass in one gulp and handed it to Satan.

"I think I'm going to need another of these," I said, and he laughed, filled the vessel and handed it back to me.

"It's okay, Michael, I've been thinking about this for a long time and it still gives me a weird feeling inside every time. It's like trying to contemplate a *true* death, where nothing exists once your soul ceases to live. It's very hard to come to terms with."

I nodded and he took it as his cue to keep going.

"So there God was, completely aware of himself and everything around him. A truly omnipotent, omniscient being, which at that stage wasn't so impressive since all that existed was Him and the elements. God knew of everything in the universe and had complete command over it; complete power."

I saw a glint in The Devil's eyes. It looked like jealousy, but it may have been something else. I couldn't be sure. He blinked and moved on.

"The Elemental became bored of just sitting in nothingness with no one to talk to. So he created the angels. The first angel he created was called Lucifer the Morning Star, which was my original name."

Satan smiled at me. "So now I can start telling you what I have seen with my own eyes, rather than what God told me happened before I was around."

"You were an angel?" I asked, aghast.

"I was until I began to question his judgment!" The Devil snarled. "But that comes later in my story. Let me proceed," he said, calming once again. I took another large sip of my drink and he continued.

"God made many angels in the beginning. He made all of us for a very simple reason, to amuse Himself. He always said that the only thing worse than having to do something is having nothing to do at all. He made us as companions to keep him happy. However, he grew weary of us quickly, for, with the exception of me, he had made all of the angels completely obedient to his will. They were like robots that could carry out his whims and wishes at the click of his fingers. This became too predictable and again He grew bored. So, God decided to create his most wonderful creature of all, one so full of ironies and imperfections that it would keep him amused forever. This creature of course was Man. The rest is the history you learnt in your bible school with Adam and Eve and the fruit that we discussed when we first met. The reason I tempted Eve to eat the fruit was that I was hooked watching them as well, and wanted to spice up the show."

"Like reality T.V." I interrupted, remembering my conversation with him in Sloth's Lounge.

"That's right," he winked. "But that's not where it ends. The world that God created was in a finite space, and it was filling up fast with human after human and every other creature He had created. It was becoming over-populated. We needed to come up with a solution to this dilemma before Earth became congested with life. After much thought and discussion, it was I who came up with the idea of death, to create space for the new life being born every day.

"At first God was against the idea of death. He said he couldn't snuff out the souls he had created, not just because he didn't want to, but because he didn't know how. He dwelt on this for a while and soon came up with the concept of Hell, to punish those who had sinned on earth, to teach them the errors of their ways and to rehabilitate them until they were fit for entry to Heaven.

"I opposed the idea of Hell from the start. I did not think that his souls deserved to be punished for exercising their right of free will, without all of God's knowledge in their heads. It was unfair. How were they supposed to make the correct decisions without all the facts? God disagreed. He only wanted the blindly obedient to sit at His side in Heaven. He didn't want the freethinkers, the intellectually curious. He didn't want the weak and the wretched; he wanted only the pure, only the sheep. We fought about this for what seemed like centuries. We fought about what we each thought was the right way to treat his grotesque children. At the end of the final argument, God ordered one of his angels to toss me down to the Hell he'd created down here, especially for the corrupted souls of earth. He then sent a messenger with instructions for me to eternally guide those wretched souls to His loving arms. God doomed me to be forever hated and outcast, while he would be forever revered and loved. It was his idea to punish them. He should have to do it! Not I, who was against the idea of Hell from the start!"

Satan's voice had risen to a shout and he was on his feet spitting the last words into the air as if in defiance at God above. Drool dripped from his chin as he bellowed the last few words and collapsed exhausted into his chair.

I sat stunned. My world had gone numb. All existence was created just to keep someone from getting bored? My life and countless others meant nothing. Everything was just a game to keep God amused. I felt as hollow as an empty coffin.

"So nothing really matters," I said, feeling hopeless.

The Devil looked up at me, clearly drained. He sunk his head into his hands and groaned.

"No. That's too nihilistic of you, Michael," he said. "Of course it all matters, everything matters. Don't you see, I've just given you the key to the meaning of life!"

"You've just told me that human life was created to pass the time!" I shouted back at him. "Me, Charlotte, everyone, we are all just pawns of entertainment to the higher powers! We are unwilling whores who please you without even knowing it. Meaningless! Meaningless! Utterly meaningless! Everything is meaningless." I was now on my feet. "We mean nothing to you and so our lives meant nothing. Our souls are now simply clogging up this stinking Hell, waiting to shuffle off to an existence of complacency in Heaven. That's not important! If that's all there is, then why bother with anything?"

The Devil looked absolutely horrified at my stream of logic. He fell from the chair he was in, onto his knees at my feet, grabbing my legs and looking up at me, pleading.

"What did you think life was?" he asked "What did you want it to mean? Think on it, Michael. Life is truly what you make if it, mortal life and beyond. If you believe it is worthless and there is no point, then life will not and cannot go on. All the feelings you have are real. Yes, there is pain and suffering, but all the joy and happiness is real as well. You must embrace your existence and enjoy it. Life is about love!" He was imploring me to understand. "Think of your love for Charlotte

121

and how right it was to you, how much it meant. But love doesn't just stop in the joys of connecting with another single soul. There is the love of what you do in every part of your life. There is the connection with friends, family and community. There is solace in the beauty of nature, rapture in physical sensations, the exhilaration of achievement. Our passion is what drives us forward; it gives us meaning by making us bigger than our personal selves. If you love everything you do and every one you know, then you have lived how God intended. He in turn loves every soul as I do. You are all his creations and His love for everyone is the same as a parent's love for any child. He may not like some of the things that you do, but God forgives and loves always. That makes life worth living, doesn't it? Knowing that no matter what you do, at the end of every day someone truly loves you, a God no less, The Creator, The God, The Elemental."

I nodded slowly in agreement. The love I felt for Charlotte still burned stronger and more real than ever. My desire for revenge was spawned from that love and, at that moment, it was my reason for pushing forward despite the pain. How we came into being was of no real consequence, but how we spent our lives together meant everything.

The Devil climbed back to his feet, smoothing the wrinkles from his suit, like he was dusting off his performance.

"I knew you would see it my way, Michael, you're too intelligent not to. Your task is still important, to you but also to me."

I looked at Satan, puzzled. "If you love God so much and all of his creations, then why do you seek to destroy him? Why would you destroy existence?"

"I would do no such thing!" he said, a wounded look distorting his face. "I want revenge on God like you, for treating me so poorly as to trap me down here against my will, but killing Him would not destroy the rest of the universe!"

"Of course it would," I retorted. "He created everything that is, so to destroy him would destroy all that is known."

The Devil scoffed at my words. "Come now, Michael, if you murder the person who built your house, it does not fall down, does it? If you imprison the man who invented the car then all cars do not cease to work! It is the same with God. If I can destroy Him, which I doubt I can, then the world would continue as if nothing had happened. Heaven would mourn for a time and then move on. My real goal is not to kill him, though. I simply want God to know what it is like to be stuck somewhere against your will and feel as I have felt for eons -- trapped. I want Him to rot in Hell and I will be free to take the throne in Heaven and hold sway over the universe. I will make things right with the world so there is less suffering than there is now. I will diminish the flow of souls to Hell and help them get to Heaven quicker. Life will be much easier with me in charge!"

He looked into space with a crazed look in his eyes that I would not do well to argue with. I would need his help if my quest were to be fulfilled. What Satan did with God after that was of no real consequence to me. I was resolute, I would triumph over Gideon. It was time I started asking the questions I needed answered if I was to succeed.

"Who is the Perceptionist?" I asked Satan. "And how can he help me?"

"You have my attention now," he said snapping out of his trance. "The Perceptionist is the most powerful being alive, equal to God. He is another Elemental."

THIRTEEN

ANOTHER ELEMENTAL? I had no idea how to respond. I just sat there with my mouth open, staring at Satan who just sat grinning back at me.

"Another?" I finally stammered.

"Yes," he replied, "another Elemental."

The silence ticked by. I still didn't know what to say next and it seemed like Satan was just waiting patiently for me to fire questions at him. Finally, it was he who broke the silence.

"He is a lot lazier than God the Elemental. He has not created any life forms, or souls or planets. He is content to sit and watch and wait, for what I'm not sure, but the Perceptionist is definitely biding his time waiting for something."

"How long?" I asked.

"He's been in existence for just over a thousand years, so he is relatively young by God's standards. He has chosen to live down in Hell for the last six hundred of those years, maybe just to make me nervous, I'm not sure. He's made no contact with me for the last three hundred of those years, nor I with him. I know he is still here because he has made no effort to conceal himself and will occasionally display his powers in plain view of the rest of Hell, simply to let us know that he is here and that he is powerful. Beyond that I know only very little."

"Then how do you know he is truly an Elemental like God? Someone who made himself come to life through sheer will?" I asked.

"Do not question my knowledge, Michael!" The Devil snarled, reminding me who I was talking with.

Satan walked over to one of the shelves and pulled a thick tome from a stack of books near the top. He threw it on the table and it landed with a muffled thud. It was one of the thickest books I'd ever seen, with a marbled, brown leather cover and stiff, yellow pages.

"This is my personal journal, Michael. I only ever write of what I deem to be significant events. So far, three of the last six entries are about things the Perceptionist has done to display his power. The first of these was to create the mountain upon which my castle now sits. He did this at my request to prove he was indeed what he claimed to be. The second display was to grow the first of Hell's buildings from the earth, which he claims to have done to better the lives of Hell's souls. The third, and final major display, was to flatten half of Hell with a click of his fingers. That was the last time I had any contact with him and I have no idea why he destroyed some of what he had made."

I opened the pages and saw Satan's spindly, handwriting scrawled over the pages. There were drawings of a being, covered from head to toe in eyes, reaching for the sky where a huge fireball formed about his head. In the next drawing, it appeared as if he had thrown the ball, and Hell City was ablaze with its light. The drawings began to move, like a living sketch. Towers crumbled, and chaos reigned as the Perceptionist stood without emotion, watching the carnage with his numerous eyes.

I looked up from the book, in awe of this being's power.

"Where is he now?" I asked.

"He now lives in a part of Hell that even I rarely visit. Aptly named Satan's Demise, it is where my biggest critics and threats reside; souls doomed to stay forever here, and who blame me for their imprisonment not God!" He was becoming angry again, but composed himself. "You must go to the Perceptionist and ask for his help according to the little nursery rhyme you brought me. I doubt he'll help you, but he is most certainly the ideal teacher if you wish to learn the mighty powers of the elements."

He sighed. "I have no idea why he should give up his time for you, though, Michael. The riddle gives no clues as to how to gain his favor."

"Of course it does!" I retorted. "Do you really think I did not memorize those verses before I handed them over to you? You think to deceive me, Satan, but you must remember we share the same goal, and it is in your interest to help me as best you can."

He took on a feigned look of hurt, pouting his lips and sulking at me. "I didn't think you would give up that easily. So tell me, what is it you think I can provide?"

I recited the poem over again in my head:

> Find the Perceptionist with a thousand eyes
> Down the yellow-door lane in Satan's Demise
> Take a gift of gold as a gift of thread
> And the eyes that belong in Phineus' head
> There you will learn the power of sight
> To create to destroy is Michael's birthright
> The Elemental's secret will soon be revealed
> And Michael's dark fate forever is sealed.

I thought for a moment before deconstructing each part to best decipher their meanings.

"Okay, so the first part," I explained to Satan, "is simply directions to find this Perceptionist. I believe the next lines are a clue to what I will have to take him in order to gain his help. The second is quite plain. You must give me Phineus' eyes to take to him."

The Devil growled in his throat, but I continued. "A gift of gold as a gift of thread is a bit harder. Do you know of a magic cloak that is made of gold?" I asked, pushing the very last line to the back of my mind. I didn't like the sound of it and so chose to ignore it, like a fool.

The Devil paused as if weighing up whether or not to help me. "The next line most likely refers to the Golden Fleece of the Argonauts. Fortunately for you, I have it in my possession," he finally said.

"Ah ha!" I exclaimed in realization, "Jason's Golden Fleece from Greek mythology! You have it?"

"I do," he said slowly. "But I don't see why The Perceptionist would want it. I think it's better if you try to get help from another demon, who doesn't have any interest in my items of value." Satan sounded like a spoiled little child.

"You must give it to me," I said, "if I'm to have any chance at all in gaining God The Elemental's secret for you, as the riddle says at the end. This is the best chance we have."

Satan's demeanor changed from one of defiance to one of grudging acceptance at my mention of God's secret.

"I don't like it," The Devil grunted. "I don't see why the Perceptionist should need such things. However, you can have both them, *if* you can pluck them from where they lie. Follow me. We shall enter my treasury."

FOURTEEN

THE DEVIL WALKED TO THE BACK WALL of the library and slid another volume from its place on the shelf, walking back with it. It was a dog-eared copy of *Treasure Island* by Robert Louis Stevenson. Satan flipped the pages open and told me to come in closer. I stood behind him, looking over his shoulder.

"Read with me," he said and began out loud, running his finger along the lines for me to follow. "I beheld great heaps of coin and quadrilaterals built of bars of gold. That was Flint's Treasure that we had come so far to seek, and that had cost already the lives of seventeen men from the Hispaniola. How many it had cost in the amassing, what blood and sorrow, what good ships scuttled on the deep, what brave men walking the plank blindfolded, what shot of cannon, what shame and lies and cruelty, perhaps no man alive could tell."

As we neared the end of the last sentence, the room around us began to shimmer and fade, warping into another realm.

The haze around me cleared to reveal a vast treasure room spanning before us. It was filled with glittering gold coins, sparkling diamonds, blood-red rubies and emeralds the color of envy. There were not only monetary riches in the hoard, but antiquities that would make any historian wet their pants upon discovering. Everything was in pristine order, meticulously maintained and sorted. Gems, precious metals and money stacked on one side of the room, while relics and items of significance sat in glass cabinets on the other. Through the middle of the treasury ran a pathway of black onyx, polished to give off a dark sheen. It ran off into the distance, about six feet wide, with aisles branching off every ten feet for easy access to each corner of the enormous cavern. It was truly breathtaking.

"What is this place? Where is this place?" I asked.

"It is everything and nothing, nowhere and everywhere," The Devil replied in an aloof tone. "It is my only real refuge from the suffocating space of Hell. It's where I come to think over problems and gain inspiration from the beautiful materials of the human world, which create most of the sin in the soul."

He stepped onto the onyx path and I fell in behind him, walking past the riches of earth: Pandora's Box, The Djinn's Lamp, Shakespeare's Original First Folio, Jimi Hendrix' last guitar. I wanted to stay in this cavern forever and explore every facet, every item. But The Devil walked on relentlessly, deeper inside.

We continued to walk along the path, which angled downward, deeper into the earth. The roof above us grew higher and higher, until it finally seemed we were out in the open air. A strange, ruddy glow was cast about the whole place, as if the walls around us lit up the chamber. The Devil walked on and on, one foot over the next, through acres of riches with me close behind. Finally he stopped. We now stood facing upwards, at a hillock, covered in the greenest grass. He pointed to the crest of the hill where a bare tree stood, skeletal and white.

"Up hanging on that tree is the golden fleece of the Argonauts," Satan said. "You will have to climb the tree to get it down. At the base of the tree lie Phineus' eyes. They can only be lifted from the ground by the virtuous of heart. Only someone with clarity of spirit, a clean soul can touch their vile jelly; namely no one who is down in Hell. You may do your best to take them from their resting place, but you will not succeed." He finished and sat down on the ground, crossing his legs and settling in, ready to enjoy the show. He clearly had nothing else to say.

I steeled myself and started to trudge up the hill. The fleece seemed easy enough. It looked like a pretty easy tree to climb. The eyes were a different story. With the amount of revenge and hatred raging in my soul, I doubted I'd be able to pick them up, *if* The Devil was speaking the truth.

As the tree came closer into view, I could see its bark was moving. Hints of brown and green shifted all over the mostly white branches and trunk, as if it was changing color to match its surroundings. The Golden Fleece hung high at the top of its branches. It twinkled with a metallic sheen, an angel on the top of a Christmas tree. It looked to me like the fleece was about the size of a bath towel, strung up flapping as if a breeze had caught it, but there was no wind on the hillock.

As I drew closer still, I realized to my horror, that the bark of the tree was not moving at all. It was covered in snakes! They writhed and twisted around the tree, slithering from top to bottom in a serpentine mass. Green, brown and red snakes flicked their devilish tongues as they stopped as one and looked at me approaching, as if they knew what I wanted to do. They watched me for a few seconds and then continued their endless circling of the tree, sliding in and out of the knots that marred its trunk and wrapped their scaly tails around small branches, hanging like bizarre fruits from a supernatural plant. I hated snakes. Everyone hates snakes! I was supposed to climb this twisted tree to get that fleece? How I would get to the top without being mauled by its guardians I was yet to figure out.

I was now at the crest of the hill and standing at the bottom of the serpent-filled tree. I reached out to touch it and a snake's head shot out at my hand, hissing and spitting venom. I leapt back as its fangs snapped shut over where my hand had just been. I looked down the hill, where I was sure I could see Satan rolling on the ground in fits of laughter. At least someone was enjoying this.

I tentatively reached forward again and another snake lunged at me, this time at my face. I caught it by the throat just before its teeth could clamp over my nose. Poison dripped from its fangs and onto the grass at my feet, which shriveled black as the venom touched. I squeezed my fist together and broke the serpent's neck. It popped inside my palm like a packet of chips.

If I could do that a few thousand more times, maybe I'd have a chance at scaling the tree and getting the fleece.

I stopped to think what I could do to get rid of those cursed snakes. I had nothing. I began to think that maybe I should try the second part of my goal first and worry about the fleece later. I searched around the base of the tree and soon saw Phineus' eyes looking up at me. They were planted among the roots, which spread out along the ground like pulsing veins. The eyes looked as if they were growing from the ground, two all seeing mushrooms rooted in the earth, pupils and cornea sitting in the centre of the bulbs at the top.

I cleared the grass from around the eyes, and bent down to see if I could pick them up. As soon as my fingers touched the closest one, a jolt of electricity flowed through my body and I was thrown clear, thumping to the ground six feet away from where I'd been standing. I struggled back to my feet and looked back at the air smoking around Phineus' eyes. It wisped up into the sky toward the fleece high in the branches. I shoved my fingers in my mouth and sucked on their charred ends. The smell of burnt hair filled my nostrils. I watched in surprise as the smoke swirled up into the air and gathered around the fleece. Snakes parted from wherever the black fog hung about the tree! As the smoke cleared, the snakes returned with renewed vigor and swarmed where there had been none, covering every inch of the white tree once more. Seeing the reaction of the snakes toward the smoke, I had an idea of how I could retrieve the fleece from the branches above.

I walked once again to where Phineus' eyes sat growing from the earth. I looked around me and found a rotting branch lying on the ground. Lifting it with my uninjured hand, I touched it to the eyes. It exploded, igniting into blue flames. I held the branch before me, at arm's length, as smoke poured from the fire that had engulfed the top end, like a torch. I waved it toward the snakes and once again they parted and slithered to the far ends of the tree they inhabited.

I moved closer still, wedged the kindling into the lowest fork of the tree and started to climb. Each branch I got to, I waved smoke around in the air to part snakes and wedged my torch in a higher branch. As my feet left each limb, snakes closed around it and seethed where my shoes had been. Slowly I made my way to the top level of the tree closest to the fleece.

Snakes poured from knots in braches, but fled as soon as I waved my fiery weapon toward them. I edged my way out toward where the fleece hung and stretched out, snagging it between my outstretched fingers then pulled it in, holding it tight to my chest. I had it! The branch I was perching on creaked menacingly. I froze. Looking down I saw the grassy earth far below; it looked soft enough, but at this height a fall would surely splinter every bone in my body to toothpicks. I slid cautiously back toward the safety of the main braches, when the worst thing possible happened. My torch went out.

FIFTEEN

SMOKE STILL STREAMED FROM THE TIP of the branch in my hand but the snakes, seeing that the flame had been extinguished, began to group around me. They hissed, flicking their tongues, no longer afraid of the smoke that had no flame to burn. I waved my weapon frantically in every direction. The serpents backed off briefly, but surged forward again as soon at the smoldering branch left their immediate space. As I swung the useless torch in one last circle, the limb holding me creaked again. The creak turned into a sickening crack, and I fell towards the ground as it gave way beneath me. Plummeting downward, I smashed and crashed into each appendage on the way, my ribs splitting like twigs, wood shattering under the momentum of my fall. The final bough broke beneath me and I tumbled to the ground with a mighty thud and rolled groaning, broken and bleeding. My ears, nose and mouth seeped death as I lay there, clutching the Golden Fleece.

I had no wind left in me. I wheezed and coughed blood as I quivered on the ground, a broken mess of mashed bones and burst organs. I rolled onto my back panting and lay looking up at the wreckage above me. The tree instantly began to knit itself back together, the snakes carrying broken branches back up the trunk to where they belonged. As the tree healed itself, I could feel my body knitting together as well. Phineus was right: "Nothing dies in Hell, Michael," he had said. Nothing dies, but everything hurt! My bones crunched as they mended themselves, my organs swelled with blood and began to pump once more, resuming normal function, but exuded throbbing, excruciating pain all through my body. The blood flowing from my ears and nose congealed, and I stopped bleeding. I still didn't move. I just lay there, gathering my wits and my breath.

I was only half way there. I had the fleece, but how would I get the eyes, Phineus' eyes? I sat up painfully and looked at the fleece in my hands, shiny and golden yet soft and warm. I would have to think laterally to get those eyes from the ground. I would have to do as Phineus had taught me. My mind ticked. I could solve this dilemma. The Devil's words echoed in my mind. *"They can only be lifted from the ground by the virtuous of heart. Only someone with clarity of spirit, a clean soul can touch their vile jelly…"*

Three words stood out to me in what he had said: virtuous, clarity, clean. Another word sprang to mind that matched those words of The Devil: purity. Only something truly pure could touch the eyes and lift them from their resting place. I looked again at the fleece resting in my hands, pure gold and pure wool. This was a symbol of absolute purity before me. This was what I would use to pluck the eyes from this demon's hill! I climbed to my feet and stumbled to the base of the tree again. I threw the fleece over the eyes. No sparks, no smoke, nothing. I was right. I felt gently through the fleece for my prize and, grasping them from the base, plucked them from the earth and wrapped them in my new golden blanket. Slinging my bundle like a sack over my shoulder, I marched in triumph back down the hill to Satan, who stood, arms crossed, at the base of the grassy knoll, waiting for my return.

"Took your time," he said sourly, his face screwed up into a ball of frustration.

Satan turned and stomped back up the onyx pathway, towards where we had first entered his treasury. As he walked up the hill, his body grew foggy. Like a ghost in the dark he faded to nothing before me. I sprinted to where he had been, but only thin wisps of moisture hung in the air where he had once stood solid. I yelled his name but there was no response. I looked around frantically for an exit; there was none. Would he leave me here to rot, I wondered. Was he so angry about me taking Phineus' eyes and the fleece? He needed me to find

Gideon's secret. Suddenly, I was struck on the head with a heavy blow. I stumbled and almost fell as I looked around to see where the attack had come from. Again I was hit, this time in the stomach, by an invisible enemy. I bent and twisted, trying to dodge my phantom attacker, but it pressed on, striking me from all sides. I heard he Devil growling in my ear, but I could not see him. I fell to the ground as I was pummeled senseless by poltergeist fists. I began to lose consciousness and everything went dark.

There was someone yelling in my ear. "Michael, wake up, Michael! We have to leave, we are no longer welcome!"

I was being shaken as I lay hurting on the ground. I forced my eyes open to see Smithy's wrinkled face looking at me. He smiled briefly when he saw I had woken. A dream, I thought, was it all a dream? I looked down and saw the Golden Fleece still wrapped in my arms.

"Michael!" Smithy shouted, jolting me back to the present. "We have to go. Satan has said we must go at once, or he'll let Moloch loose on us again. What did you do to make him so angry?"

"I won this from him," I said showing him the fleece. His eyes went wide as he noticed it for the first time, cradled in my arms.

"No wonder he's so furious!" Smithy said, "I remember what he went through to get that when I was in his employ. It was the last time he ever went to Satan's Demise. I'm sure he didn't give it up easily."

The pain wracking every fiber in my body was testament to that, but I chose to remain silent on the subject. Instead all I said was, "Let's get out of here!"

Smithy sprang to his feet and dragged me up with him.

"Follow me!" he said and darted out of the library we were in. I pursued him through the art-lined passages and burst out of a side door into the sweltering heat of Hell. Smithy's helicopter sat ahead, repaired and polished. We wasted no time and climbed aboard. Smithy fired up the engines. The blades whirred and we lifted off into the air.

"If I never see this damned place again it will be too soon!" Smithy yelled as we surged down the mountain back towards his airfield, looking behind us the whole way for The Devil's red dragon. Thankfully, we saw nothing of him.

"I didn't get to gather any intelligence on the mission. Sorry, Sir," Smithy said gravely as we as we touched down. "I was consumed with my haunting of guilt while you were gone. I've failed you, Sir." He hung his head and pulled the money I'd paid him from out of his pocket and handed it back to me. This was really a noble man. I couldn't believe he deserved to be trapped down in Hell. I handed the notes back to him, smiling.

"You did more than your share of work for the mission, Smithy. I got what I came for," I said, holding up the fleece. His worried look turned back to a friendly smile as I beamed at him.

"I'm glad you succeeded, Sir," he said and we climbed down from the chopper and walked back to his office.

Mack sat on a chair leaning against the outside wall of Smithy's shed. His feet rested on the bonnet of his taxi as he read a newspaper called Hell's Clarion. He folded the paper down as we approached, and looked over the top.

"Hi boys, I hope you had fun up there!" he said, lazily climbing to his feet. "You get what you want?"

I patted my bundle in answer. He let a low whistle escape from his teeth as he saw the glitter of gold in my hands.

"Well then, buddy, you'll be wanting to go somewhere else, I suppose?" he asked.

"To Satan's Demise," I replied.

PART THREE
SATAN'S DEMISE

ONE

"YOU'VE GOT TO BE BLOODY JOKING, wanting to go to Satan's Demise!" Mack said, in shock.

"No joke," I said. "You can't handle a simple cab fare downtown? I thought you were a tough guy, but I guess I was wrong."

"But it's Satan's Demise!" he stammered, before pulling himself together. "Well, I guess it's not that bad," he said in a deliberately deep voice. "Jump in and I'll have you there in two shakes of a rattle-snake's tail." I shuddered at the mention of snakes and turned to bid Smithy farewell.

"You did a fine job, Captain," I said seriously. "Thank you, sir and I'll be back again if I require your special services." I mentioned nothing of why he was in Hell. He seemed a happier soul when he wasn't thinking about it.

"Not too soon, I hope!" he said as he shook my hand. I smiled at the old man in front of me. I wondered if those were really just wrinkles on his face, rather than deep tear tracks etched into his skin from a lifetime of sadness.

"Not too soon," I promised sincerely. I slowly tore my eyes away from him and turned back to Mack.

"Do you know where the Perceptionist lives?" I asked.

Mack's eyes almost popped out of his head at the mention of the powerful Elemental. His face drained of all color.

"I can take you to the foot of his lane-way," Mack managed to say weakly. "After that, you're on your own."

"That's all I need," I said and jumped into the passenger seat of Mack's now clean taxi.

"All I need, he says; frickin' nut case, gonna get me killed," I heard Mack mumble as he walked around to the driver's door and got inside. He looked at me again before shaking his head and starting the car. As we rolled out of the driveway, Smithy waved furiously, smiling and shouting for us to visit and have a cup of tea next time we were in the area.

We screeched back out onto Hell's Highway and settled into the chaotic traffic, cars roaring around us.

"You must have gone to a lot of trouble to get that," Mack said nodding toward the fleece in my lap.

"You have no idea," I said.

"I hope she's worth it," Mack said as he drove. I snapped my head around to face him, furious.

"Excuse me?" I snarled.

"Whoa, buddy," he said, holding up his hands in self-defense. "It was only an observation. Men only ever go to so much trouble when there's a gal involved." She must be a special one if you're going to the devil's door for her. I'm sure she's worth every breath you spend on her."

"Every breath and more," I said, breaking off the conversation. I looked out the window as we drove onwards. Mack took the hint and remained silent. He could tell I wasn't in the mood for small talk. I sank into deep thought about how much I loved my Lotte; how much she had loved me.

I lay in my bed next to Charlotte. She rolled over sleepily and smiled at me.

"What are you looking at?" she yawned.

"The most beautiful girl on earth," I replied truthfully . She blushed and rolled back over, closing her eyes again. Lotte was never able to take a compliment on her beauty. She was always completely oblivious to how attractive she was. I snuggled up into her, hugging her close to my body. She fit every curve of me. We locked together like pieces of a jigsaw. It struck me how perfect we were for each other. We didn't only match mentally, but physically as well.

I leaned in and whispered into her ear, "I love you."

"I love you too, Michael," she said sleepily.

I watched her as she fell back to sleep. She was so innocent, so perfect. Nothing would ever change that in my mind.

I was brought to the present by the click-click of Mack's indicator, as we drove off an exit ramp that read *Satan's Demise*. It wouldn't be long now, I thought. My mind turned to Gideon. I could see his mocking smile in my mind, evil and pious. I would wipe that smirk from his face when next we met. I would smash his perfect cheek-bones with my knuckles and peel his flesh from him in strips. I would avenge my love. I would make him cry out to the devil to make me stop. Then, I would tear him up some more. Hatred filled my soul to the brim as I thought of that bastard. I hoped that this Perceptionist had the darkest and most brutal of powers to give me, so I could unleash them on the monster that took her from me.

I looked up from my reverie and saw that we were now in the heart of Satan's Demise. The constant red glow from the sky threw ominous shadows around the ransacked buildings and crumbling shacks that lined the street. There were no electric lights, apart from the yellow glow coming from the headlights of our cab, which shone upon the broken windows and cracked walls of the dark suburb. The streets were deserted, not a soul, human or demon to be seen. I almost expected tumbleweed to come rolling down the street at any minute. Every now and then, I swear I the saw green dots of a cat's eyes glowing at me from out of some of the abandoned buildings that lined the street.

Mack slowed his cab to a crawl, the wheels crunching broken glass underneath us as we came to a stop. Mack looked at me.

"Better sit tight for a moment," he said looking at his watch. "It's just about time for The Guilt."

I was about to explain that Satan had spared me the visions, but I stopped myself. What would my friend think of me if he knew I was working with The Devil?

I could hear it coming before I saw it. The rushing and growling fires of Hell, rumbled towards us as we sat in the dark. The flames hit our cab with a loud bang. We rocked back and forth, as I watched Mack close his eyes and begin convulsing heavily. Tears began streaming down his face and sobs wracked his body.

"I'm so sorry," he screamed over and over.

The sight of such a burly looking man crying made me feel deep sympathy for him.

"I didn't mean it," he wailed. "No, I'm sorry, it's not like that."

Mack was holding his arms out in pleading as his whole body lurched and shuddered in his seat.

"I love you. I don't love her. I wish I could take it back," he blubbered loudly as the fire swept over the cab.

I looked away from him. He was obviously remembering a time when he cheated on his girlfriend or wife. Here was another soul who was punishing himself for his wrongs on earth, unable to forgive himself his weaknesses. I wondered if he would ever let his guilt go and pass over to Heaven. It was heart wrenching to see someone so strong in life look so helpless and pitiful while The Guilt took hold of him.

The fire began to subside around us. I leaned back in my seat and closed my eyes, pretending to be experiencing guilt of my own. Mack slowly stopped crying next to me. I heard him wiping away his tears before shaking me awake.

"Michael," he said, "It's over, Michael, wake up."

I slowly opened my eyes to look at Mack. He still had tears streaked over his face, despite his efforts to conceal them. He looked away from me across the road to our right with glassy eyes. Clearing his throat he mumbled, "I think we're here."

I followed his gaze and saw that we had stopped at the front of a long, gloomy laneway, which had a single globe at the end lighting an insipid, yellow doorway.

"That's it," I blurted upon seeing the door. "This is where I get out." I moved to exit the cab, not wanting to face Mack after watching such a private moment of grief without him knowing it. I felt like a liar.

"Michael, before you go," Mack said earnestly. "This Perceptionist ain't no push over demon. This guy is the real deal. Don't go in there unless you really need to."

I was moved at his concern for someone who was practically a stranger.

"I need to," was all I said. He looked in my eyes and nodded.

"Well, good luck then, pal, I hope I see you again in one piece."

I pulled the remaining cash from my pocket and gave it to Mack.

"I don't think I'll be needing this anymore," I said. He tried to give it back to me; I simply dropped the bills on the seat as I got up and stepped out onto the pitch-black street.

"Good luck," Mack said again, leaning out the window. "If you ever get out of this joint alive, look me up. There's something about you I like."

"I will," I said, smiling for the first time since I got in the cab. "I like you too Mack."

I turned and started down the alleyway without looking behind me. I heard Mack's cab roll slowly away and focused on the door at the end of alley. The light above the door flickered and I caught movement in the shadows ahead. A voice boomed out at me.

"Who dares come to the lair of the Perceptionist? Reveal yourself and your purpose or I shall cut you down."

I heard the distinct sound of ringing metal and saw the flash of a long blade being pulled from its scabbard. I could see the shining sword, but not the being that held it in the darkness. I stopped, deciding to reveal who I was. If this Perceptionist was the powerful, all-knowing being he was supposed to be, then he already knew I was coming.

"My name is Michael," I said into the shadows. "I come with a gift for the Perceptionist. I come seeking knowledge." In the darkness, I saw white teeth spread into a smile.

"Hello, Michael!" the voice called from the shadows. A tall, bearded African man stepped into the light, lowering his weapon to the ground. "We've been expecting you."

"Marlowe?" I cried, taken aback at seeing the man I'd met in the Prophet Casino the day before. "What are you doing here?"

"I'm employed by the Perceptionist to keep him safe from intruders," he said. I had instant respect for the man in front of me. Marlowe must be an extremely dangerous and cunning person to be working for such a being as his personal bodyguard. He slid his blade back into a scabbard strapped to his back, and thrust his hand out in greeting. I shook it strongly.

"You're lucky I know your face," he said. "Normally, I lop off heads and ask questions later."

"I guess I'm lucky to have met you in that bar, then," I replied.

"More like fate than luck," he said. "A few hours after I met you, I also met the man you were looking for, Phineus. He is a very interesting character."

"Phineus!" I started, suddenly full of questions. "Where did you meet him? Is he okay? What happened to him after I had the visions? Do you know where he is now?"

"Relax, my friend," Marlowe said soothingly. "You can ask him all of this yourself. He is inside."

TWO

"INSIDE?" I blurted at Marlowe. "What has Phineus got to do with the Perceptionist?" I asked, stunned.

"Let's go and ask him," Marlowe replied simply, turning around and opening the yellow door.

He waved for me to go inside and followed me into a perfectly square room. All of the walls were painted the same yellow as the door we'd just come through. I heard the door shut. Looking behind, it was completely gone. Just a smooth wall stood in its place. We were now in this fever yellow room with no apparent way in or out. I was completely disoriented and confused.

"Where to now?" I asked Marlowe.

"Through that doorway," he said, pointing at a solid wall.

"There's no door there," I said, exasperated.

"Well, that depends on your perception then, doesn't it," he replied smiling and walked over to the wall. I followed closely, and as he got to the wall, he walked right through. I tried to walk through the space he had just disappeared through but hit hard against solid wood, smacking my nose painfully. I stumbled backwards, shocked. Marlowe's head appeared through the wall again, smiling from ear to ear.

"Look at it as if you know there is a doorway there," he said.

"What is this? A Harry Potter movie?" I asked Marlowe. He looked at me, puzzled.

I stood back and concentrated on the wall. Nothing happened. I must have frowned because Marlowe came back through the wall and stood with me.

"You must know it is there, not just think it's there," he said. "You must truly believe there is a door and it will appear."

145

I stepped forward again. Logically there must be a door there if Marlowe could step through it, I reasoned. It didn't matter that my eyes couldn't see the porthole. As soon as I came to this conclusion, a black doorway appeared on the wall, growing from the center and framed itself to another room, where I could see Phineus. He was sitting at a table talking to a man who rocked back and forth, cross-legged on the floor in the corner of the room.

"Phineus!" I called. He turned his blind eyes my way and waved.

"Come in, Michael," he said, "now that you can see the way." I walked through the doorway and took a seat next to him. Marlowe walked in behind me and stood quietly in the corner, next to the rocking man.

"I see you've brought my eyes and fleece," Phineus said. Once again, it struck me as ironic that a blind man was talking about seeing things.

"Your fleece?" I asked shocked. "I was under the impression it was to be the Perceptionist's fleece. What the hell happened to you anyway, what happened while I had the visions you gave me?" Phineus looked at his feet as if ashamed.

"I'm sorry, Michael," Phineus said. "I haven't been completely honest with you. When I said I could show you the best way to getting what you wanted I was speaking the truth. However, I didn't tell you this path would benefit me greatly also."

"What do you mean?" I asked coldly. I hated the thought of being manipulated by anyone, including the blind man in front of me.

"You'll soon realize why I couldn't let you know the full details, but I'll start from the beginning," he said. I remained silent and he continued.

"When you told me that you'd been sent by Satan, I had to look in your heart to make sure that your intent was not of his doing, but of your own volition. Once I'd divined that you were speaking the truth, I envisioned the best path for you to take in completing your vengeful task. To my surprise, this path involved me greatly, but who am I to go against what fate wishes? So, I showed you what you needed to know."

I sat with my arms crossed, ready for more lies.

"I saw that you would need tuition from the most powerful of beings in Hell, the Perceptionist, but that he would not help you unless I convinced him," he continued. "How I would do this was by promising to teach him the power of foresight, one power The Perceptionist does not possess. I could not teach him properly without the use of my own eyes. I need to see whom I am teaching, and where he is focusing his energies. I could not do this with my inner eye alone, so I sent you to retrieve my physical eyes from Satan. The Golden Fleece was a bonus, since I knew you would have to acquire it in order to pluck my eyes from the base of the serpent tree."

"Why didn't you just tell me this?" I fumed.

"I could not," he answered back. "If I had have told you why you needed my eyes, The Devil would not have given them to you. He would never assent to the Perceptionist gaining more power than he already has."

"I wouldn't have told him if you said to get it secretly," I snapped.

"You wouldn't have had to tell him, Michael. You are aware he can read a soul's deepest secrets while down in his domain. Otherwise he would not be able to do the job he was sent down here to do."

"But the blood, your blood was all over the room when I awoke," I said confused.

"Oh that," he said waving it away as if it was nothing. "My eye sockets always bleed when I experience visions," he explained. "Visions as intense as the ones I showed you cause me to spurt blood from my optic nerve. You were knocked unconscious by the power of what you saw. This is why, by the time you woke, I was gone. While I bled, you slept, exhausted from the experience. I wrote the note that you found pinned to the door so it would lead you to where you are now. I'm glad I was right."

I sat silent for a moment, taking in all he'd just told me. It was all a ruse. I turned the events of the past two days over in my head. I accepted it all quietly, coming to the conclusion that it could not have been done any other way. I was where I needed to be. It seemed fate was working for me so far. I wondered if I could have possibly taken another path and still ended up in the same place if this was really where fate wanted me. I pushed that puzzle to the back of my mind for later; this was not the time for wondering, it was a time for revenge.

"So, is this the Perceptionist?" I asked, indicating the rocking man that Marlowe stood over in the corner. Phineus snorted with laughter, while Marlowe said nothing.

"This is not the Perceptionist by any means," Phineus said. "This is his old apprentice, Germaine. He was a lot like you in the beginning, strong of spirit and purpose, maybe not so strong of mind. The Perceptionist set out to teach him how to see the universe in a different light and control the elements around him. To help gain a different perspective on things, Germaine began to take many strange substances. He did this in order to expand his mind and gain an altered perception of reality. At first he learned incredible things and saw many ideas from an open view. His mind began to grow, but soon he took too many of the drugs and his mind expanded too quickly; his coherent thoughts were lost inside its expanse.

"Germaine's ideas started to echo around the prism of cells in his skull, creating strange voices. He began to listen to these echoes of thoughts, believing them to be wise beings, and he was lured into false thinking. The voices told him to act and he did; they told him to ignore the instructions of the Perceptionist and take his own path. Soon he was following orders from an echo of an echo and became a shadow of his

148

real self. His purpose faded away along with his brain and now Germaine sits in the corner of this dark room, just a shell of himself, void, catatonic, empty.

"The Perceptionist leaves him here to serve as a warning to others: that an expanded perspective on reality is nothing, if you lose sight of the reality you began with."

I looked at the dribbling husk of a man in front of me and felt nothing but pity. I wondered if the person he was fighting for in the first place had any idea of his fate. I wondered if Charlotte knew up there in limbo what I was doing for her. Of course she knew, I decided. She surely understood I would do everything in my power to make everything right for us. Phineus cleared his throat loudly in his chair, and my attention was brought back to the room around me.

"May I please have my eyes now?" he asked.

I saw no point in keeping them from him any longer, and so handed him the fleece with his precious lobes wrapped inside. He unwrapped the bundle gently and carefully picked up his eyes. He lifted the bandage from his face, exposing the ghastly bleeding sockets beneath, before slowly placing his eyeballs back where they belonged. Phineus shrieked in pain as the veins of his eyes knitted back together and the nerves reconnected themselves. Falling to the ground, clutching his face, he writhed on the floor. I bent to help him but he waved me back, panting. The pain had stopped. The prophet Phineus was whole again. He wobbled to his feet and opened his eyes for the first time in over two thousand years. His eyelids were caked in blood, the red lids framing the strangest of eyes, powder-blue with clouds of white inside them, as if they reflected the skies of Heaven. No wonder The Devil thought they were the source of his power.

Phineus looked around the room, smiling. "I forgot how beautiful the world is," he said.

I looked around the room, and what he was looking at: a table, a chair and grey walls. Hardly beautiful, but I guess even

149

the simplest things become beautiful when you have been deprived of sight for so long. I gave Phineus a moment to take in his re-found vision, but I couldn't wait long before I brought up the topic of my training again.

"Phineus, have you spoken to the Perceptionist about me and what I need?" I asked.

He dragged his eyes from the golden hilt of Marlowe's sword.

"Oh yes, I've spoken to him at great length about you, Michael," he answered in a mysterious tone. "He's ready to begin your training as soon as you are ready. He has accepted my terms that he must first successfully teach you the power of the elements before I show him how to tap into the unknown future." Phineus turned back to the African standing in the corner.

"Marlowe, if you please, we'd like to enter your master's chamber," he said.

Marlowe nodded and stepped back. A swirling blue portal opened in the corner behind him.

"Step through, Michael. Phineus, you must wait here with me until the Perceptionist has had an audience with Michael alone."

Phineus nodded as if he had expected as much, and pushed me lightly on the back, urging me forward. I stepped past Marlowe into the glowing portal. Lacerating cold cut through my skin, like I was being blasted by a thick arctic wind. I closed my eyes to protect them from freezing solid. I pushed through the chilling air blindly. It was thick and textured against my body, almost like I was trying to walk underwater. I stumbled forward as the condensed air gave way to a thin feeling of nothingness. The shock of cold was immediately replaced with an overall feeling of warmth. I opened my eyes and almost fell over in shock. I now stood face to face with the most bizarre creature I had ever witnessed. I had no doubt in my mind that this was the entity I had been searching for.

THREE

"WELCOME," the being in front of me whispered lightly. I studied it. I was quite sure it had no sex at all, it appeared purely androgynous. I guess because I'm male, I've since referred to the Perceptionist as him, but I'm positive a female would say 'her' instead.

The creature was about twice my size in every dimension, shaped like a giant human but with no hair at all on his body. He had five eyes on his face, two on each side, one above the other and a fifth in the dead-center where his nose would have been, if he had one. It was exactly like the number five side of a dice. Each eye blinked separately every few seconds. His mouth was where a normal human's would have been, but it was without teeth or lips. It was just a slit that moved when he talked. His skin was as white as leprosy and almost completely covered in tattoos. The tattoos were of more eyes, all a uniform size and shape; each a different color. He was a walking rainbow of tattooed eyes.

The strangest thing of all was that these tattoos blinked and looked around the room at me as normal eyes would. I'm sure each eye was seeing a different side of me, seeing all emotion, all feelings and all thoughts. I stared, awestruck at this unique alien in front of me. He had created his own body and this was how he made himself, constructed out of the elements. I studied him and he studied me back, saying nothing for minutes on end, his eyes blinking, shutting and opening in a flurry all over his body. The Perceptionist slowly walked around me; his movements were completely fluid and agile, which seemed strange for someone so large. As he lifted his legs to move, he pointed his toes and arched his legs in a pronounced, graceful stride. He completed a full circle around me and then spun around himself so I could look at him fully. It was a strange ritual, as if he wanted me to see every part of him for what it was, to become accustomed to him. From behind he looked exactly the same as the front. The same face and eyes. So many eyes. His elbows and knees appeared to be absolutely double jointed because they bent slightly towards me no matter which way he was facing. Finally, he stopped his display and looked at me, every eye now open and fixed on mine.

"So, Michael, you've come to learn the power of the elements to avenge your love, dooming yourself to an eternity in Hell," he said.

"You are right about learning power and revenge," I answered very slowly, not wanting to offend him somehow with a hasty answer or jerky movement. "However," I continued, "I don't plan on a life in Hell. I plan on reuniting with my love once my revenge is complete."

A strange noise came from the Perceptionist's mouth -- it sounded like birds chirping. I wasn't sure but I thought it was the sound of him laughing.

"I sense that you are afraid of me," the Perceptionist said. He was right, I was petrified. "It is only understandable to be afraid of what we don't understand," he continued soothingly. "But be sure that I do not mean to harm you in any way or you would have been negated in the alleyway outside. I am here to teach you. Phineus has told me of your destiny and the role you need me to play. In order to do this the way I wish, you must trust me completely. I can see your entire past mapped out behind you, so there is no need to explain reasons for your purpose. Now, you must take my word as truth. If you question this you will not be able to see what I see and, therefore, you will not able to wield the power I wield. Do you understand? Good." He finished before I could answer. "Now look around you and explain to me what you see."

152

"I see nothing," I said, as we were indeed standing in nothingness. I was not standing on ground or positioned anywhere inside a room. All around us was nothing, it was not even a color, not even black, it was just a void. It was much stranger to have nothing around me than to be in some of the bizarre settings I'd experienced in Hell.

"This is what I saw when I first woke up," the Perceptionist said, apparently referring to when he spawned himself into consciousness.

"There was nothing around me. I floated in space, out in the deepest reaches of the universe that God, The Elemental before me had neglected to touch. At first I thought I was blind, so I grew myself as many eyes as I could fit onto my skin in order to be able to perceive the unperceivable. Eventually, I learned to see the things around me, the particles that made up the nothingness. These are the elements. They are everything. You will need to learn to see these before we can move forward with your training. Now sit down and relax," he said.

Even though there was no floor to sit on, I sat, and the Elemental did the same in front of me. He closed all of the eyes on his body accept the one in the middle of his face and stared at me. I stared back.

"You must look around you and see the tiniest points of light swirling all around us. There are particles of every possible shape and color, all smaller than specks of dust, but they can be fused together to create larger elements, like building blocks. By piecing the elements together you can make anything you desire: fire, wind, water and earth; also spirit, emotion and intelligence. To harness the power of the elements is to harness all the power in the universe."

I accepted what he was saying. It made sense to me that this was more than possible; that these elements existed was probable. My rudimentary knowledge of atoms from high-school science classes made it easy for me to envisage that there were elements swirling all around me. I stared and stared into the space, looking for something, anything. Nothing appeared. The Perceptionist sat still.

"You are close," he said. "But you are trying too hard. You are trying to see something that is right in front of you, it should be evident that these elements are real. The elements aren't hidden away or concealed by objects. They *are* the objects. Now fix onto your breathing and believe in what I'm saying and you will see them."

I blinked slowly, breathing in deeply, filling my lungs and then exhaling loudly. I knew this creature was telling the truth, I believed it with all my heart. I began to see a faint glow, a general light at first, but as I looked closer I began to see separate points of light all around. It was like looking at a galaxy of stars take shape through a telescope.

"Excellent!" the Perceptionist said, laughing his strange sound of birds again. "You already learn faster than any being I've ever taught, which, of course, is only to be expected considering your paternity."

I sat up more alert than ever. I was an orphan with no idea who my mother or father was. I was told that my mother was a prostitute who had fallen pregnant to a client and had handed me over to the nuns after my birth. Other than that I knew nothing.

"You are right about your mother," the Perceptionist said, interrupting my thoughts just as The Devil had done. "Your father is a different story," he said.

"You know who my father is?" I asked quickly. As a child I dreamed he was someone rich and famous who would one day come to rescue me from my poor life.

"Your father is rich," he said reading my thoughts once again. "And he is most definitely famous."

I couldn't believe what I was hearing. My whole life had been spent wondering where I had come from, what my family history really was.

"Who is he?" I demanded. "Can I meet him? Where is he?"

The Perceptionist looked at me without expression.

"Your father is down in Hell, Michael. You have met him already."

Already met him? I thought, perplexed. Was it Mack, or Smithy?

"No," the Perceptionist said slowly. "Your father is Satan."

FOUR

I JUMPED TO MY FEET, shouting. "Liar, you're a liar! Satan is not my father!"

The instant these words escaped from my lips, the elemental lights went out around me and we stood in nothingness once more.

"Why should I lie to you?" he said innocently. "I've told you that you must trust what I say and that I will never break that trust. You must learn to accept even the most impossible truths if you are to harness the power I can teach you."

"This is a lie!" I said again, stomping around furiously in the void of nothingness. I felt like my soul had been sucked out of my body. I was empty. This couldn't be. Why was he telling me this?

"I knew you would reject what I have said at first, but you must concede that it makes perfect sense," the Perceptionist said firmly. "Why else would the Devil trust you with learning God's secret from Gideon? Why else would he send you to succeed where he failed? Why else would God send Gideon to kill you and banish you to Hell, if you were just a normal human? He made sure your heart was full of rage when you died so you wouldn't go to Heaven and spread Satan's seed where it isn't wanted. You have not thought about these things hard enough because of your rage, your blind need for revenge. Think on it now and accept the truth of it."

It was hard to argue with the logic of a supreme being, but I refused to accept it. It was true that all of these questions were answered by the possibility that The Devil was my father. There had to be another answer.

"Why didn't Satan tell me this himself?" I asked, grasping for a sense of reason.

"There was no immediate benefit to him," The Elemental continued. "In fact, it would have simply wasted valuable time in you getting to Gideon. If he had told you right away there would have been questions that needed answering and painful realization on your part; all of these things take time. Satan knows that Gideon is gaining strength by the day and if God were to find out your plan, he would never leave him unguarded on earth. Once The Devil had the secret safely in his hands he would have told you and recruited your help in defeating God."

I shook my head in denial, but could think of nothing to counter the argument. The Perceptionist realized his advantage and pressed on.

"The other reason I am telling you is because I believe this knowledge will help with your confidence in learning the knowledge of the elements. It is a positive, from my point of view. If you know that your blood is of a higher being, then you can accept more readily your ability to control these powers. The mind is the most powerful thing in the world as long as you believe in its power. Of course, Satan will be angry that you found out from me, but that is not my concern," he added. "You must accept this truth before we can move on. I have no reason to lie to you, Michael. How would that benefit me? You cannot deny it, so accept it. I understand it's difficult, but give in to the possibility and you will realize it's fact. Your human reaction of denial is a waste of time and energy."

I began to acknowledge that the Perceptionist was indeed telling the truth, even if it was a hard thing to bear. I was the son to the most hated being in the entire universe. I was the anti-Christ.

I sat down, staring into space. What did this truly mean? Did it mean I was evil? Did Satan being my father affect my current course of rescuing my love? No. Lotte was more important than anything. I couldn't ignore this revelation, but for now dwelling on it would serve no purpose.

Another realization dawned on me. The Perceptionist had confirmed the possibility that God had a hand in murdering Lotte and me. Before, I had only really been concerned with bringing Gideon to justice; now God would taste my vengeance as well. As I accepted the truth of the Perceptionist's words, the lights of the elements returned around me.

"Why would you aid me if you know that, should I succeed in gaining Gideon's secret, God may be doomed?" I asked.

"His fate is of no consequence to me," the Perceptionist said flatly. "Phineus has said if I help you, he will teach me to see into the future, to know the unknown. It is more power that I seek, and knowledge is power. The better question is: why would Phineus help you? I believe he also resents God's freedom while he himself is trapped in Hell. I think he wants revenge on God just as you and Satan do," he finished.

Again, it made sense. I was still coming to terms with the fact that I knew who my father was, but I had even more pressing matters at hand than my father. The all-consuming need for revenge was still boiling deep inside me.

"Is it possible to trap God?" I asked. If anyone would know then it would be the creature in front of me.

"Of course it is possible," he said, chirping his bird's laugh.

"But how do you trick an omnipotent being?" I asked. "It seems impossible that if he is all powerful and all knowing that anything could contain him."

"Omnipotence is an illusion," the Perceptionist explained. "Let me ask you a question to help you better understand. Could God make a wall so strong that He himself could not break it?"

"If he is all powerful then he could," I answered, without giving it too much thought.

"Ah, but if he was all powerful then wouldn't he be able to break the wall after He had made it? Either He can make it unbreakable or He can't. Both outcomes end in God not being

158

able to achieve something. Therefore, it is impossible for him to be all powerful. The same can be applied with knowledge. Can God create a puzzle that He doesn't know the answer to?"

My mind was spinning but I understood what he was saying.

"So you believe God has created something He cannot break or know. Could that be the secret that Gideon is holding?" I wondered.

"Very good!" the Perceptionist said, clapping his hands together. "You do learn fast. I can see you will become very powerful, very quickly. It is most likely that God has created a prison for Himself somewhere, and that Gideon is the holder of the key to that prison. He may also have the knowledge of where it is located. I do not know this, of course, for God does have the power to mask His secrets from even me, but I think it is probable. Why God would make such a prison is the biggest puzzle to me. Knowing God, he likely did it just to see if he could, and now cannot destroy it because he succeeded completely."

The possibility of God having created a prison for Himself provided me with some much needed hope, and hope was all I had right now. If the Perceptionist was right, then I'd be able to take my revenge on not only Gideon, but his master as well. I'd need to learn the power of the elements completely if I was to succeed as I wished. I settled myself back down on the ground and pushed all thought from my mind. The startling revelation of Satan being my father would have to wait until next we met. At that moment, all I wanted to do was learn how to destroy my enemies.

"Let's begin," I said determinedly to the Perceptionist.

FIVE

LOOKING THROUGH THE MILLIONS of points of light, I could just make out the figure of the Perceptionist. He was sitting mere inches away from me, but the galaxy of elements between us made the distance seem greater. His voice rang out clearly through the dazzling spectacle.

"You must learn to shut out the elements that you don't need to see," he said. "At times it will be best to shut them all out completely. If you're creating fire then focus only on the fire elements and the rest will dissipate. The same goes for the rest of the elements. I'll now show you how to differentiate between each of the different kinds of elements. It is a matter of color."

With a wave of his hand, the Perceptionist swept all the lights between us so I could see him properly. He proceeded to open and close certain eyes all over his body, while looking at and picking out elements from around him, placing them in order in the space between us. Each separate element hung still in the spot he had placed it. In all, there were over a hundred elements in front of us. Four in particular stood larger than the rest, at the top of the grid he had created. Red, blue, brown and green.

"Fire, air, earth and water," he said, pointing each one out respectively. "These are the most simple to master and the only elements you'll need to defeat Gideon. The others will take centuries for you to control properly, if ever."

He then motioned to the elements underneath the main four. "These are the elements that make up the human soul when arranged in perfect order. They include all of the emotions, spirit, free will and the different types of intelligence. Arrange the master elements of air, fire, earth and water together in the right way, and you create body. Add both body and soul together and you have life as we know it on Earth."

As he explained this, he built mini diagrams with the lights to show what he meant. He built a miniature human body and fused it with a glowing golden soul. They flashed brightly and the little man began walking around. Before the miniature walked too far, the Perceptionist waved the elements apart and the man was no more.

"Enough of that for now, Michael," the Perceptionist said. "We must work on the elements that will help you in your quest." He swept all but the master elements from between us.

I focused on the four points of light that remained in front of me, taking in each one's unique color and shape.

"We will start with fire first," the Perceptionist said.

He picked out the red fire element, and brought more like it from around him to hang in the space between us. He linked them together in a thick loop, attaching each single element together by pinching them in his fingers. They stuck together as if they belonged that way to begin with.

"Now, shut your eyes and concentrate on seeing as you would normally see the world, through human eyes," he instructed.

I shut my eyes and thought about what the void and the Perceptionist looked like the first time I came through the portal. I slowly opened my eyes and beheld the void as it should be, except a large ring of blazing fire hung in the air in front of me. I blinked because of its brightness.

"You made that fire from nothing!" I exclaimed.

"No, I made it from the elements," he corrected. "Alone they are too small to be of any significance, but arranged in just the right way they can create whatever you set your mind to."

He waved his hand and the fire dispersed into sparks that faded into the void. I was in wonder at the power I'd just witnessed. I saw the eternal potential in what the Perceptionist had just done. Once I mastered the elements, I could achieve anything imaginable!

"Now you must try. Return your perspective to see the elements of fire," he said.

I shifted my focus and the red points of light returned around me, floating and spinning in every direction. The Perceptionist held his hand up and they stopped moving.

"I will make it as easy as possible for the first try," he said. "Now pick one up."

I reached out to catch one of the tiny sparks. It eluded my grasp, slipping from my fingers every time I tried to pinch them from the air. I began to grow frustrated and the Perceptionist stopped me.

"Don't grab them, or pinch them like an oaf," he said sternly. "It's more like lifting an eyelash off someone's cheek. You almost have to let the element stick to your finger rather than actually take a hold of it. This requires finesse."

As he finished the sentence he plucked five fire elements from the air, each sticking to a separate finger on his hand. He made it look so easy. I felt stupid for not being able to do it. He then curled his fingers into his palm and opened it to reveal a large single element of fire. I'm sure if I was looking with a normal point of view I would have seen a flame flickering in his hand.

"Try again," he said; throwing the elements away like they were nothing.

I reached out slowly again, focusing on one element right in front of me. I pressed my forefinger to it lightly and it stuck. An involuntary laugh escaped from my lips. The Perceptionist's mouth turned up into a creepy smile. I used the other fingers on my hand to trap other elements of fire before pressing them together in my palm as he had shown me. They stuck together immediately, and formed a larger red blob in my hand. I did this seven times and then stuck the blobs together to make a solid mass the size and shape of a tennis ball. I shifted my focus back so I could witness my handy work. A brilliant fireball hung above my hand in the air. It didn't burn me, but I could feel its heat. I grasped it and launched it out into the void where it faded away in the distance.

"That's why I'm teaching you this here," the Perceptionist said. "If you'd done that in my home, you would have burnt the place down!" The bird chirping noise escaped his lips again, and I realized he had just made a joke.

"Teach me more," I whispered, dizzy with power. "Teach me much more."

SIX

THE PERCEPTIONIST TAUGHT ME in the void for what seemed like months on end. There was no day or night to calculate the passing of time. I slept when I was tired and practised obsessively every waking moment. I would concentrate on a particular element at a time. My favorite was fire. It was like a liquid to deal with, flowing and rushing where I directed it, cascading through the void under my will. I had become a master of the inferno. It was time to test my powers.

I surveyed the scene before me, a scene the Perceptionist had made from the elements. This was a training ground; a forest of dangers suspended in nothingness. My teacher stood at my shoulder, whispering in my ear.

"There is only fire, earth, air and water in that forest, Michael. The monsters contained within are just shells, they are not truly alive. Have no fear in scattering them into dust, for they are meaningless. You must pass through this jungle to the other side if you want me to teach you the power of flight."

I steeled myself to move through the gauntlet. I had to make it from one end to the other in one piece, using my new skills to preserve myself. My reward at the end would be the knowledge of how to soar like a bird.

"Remember, Michael," The Perceptionist coached, "you needn't touch the elements now to command them. Pull them around you with the power of your mind. They will bend to your will if you command them with certainty. Now go!"

With the utmost conviction, I gathered air behind my back and pushed myself into a run. I could see no easy entrance into the dense scrub so I sent a burst of fire to open a path before me. Blazing ahead, the flame ate through the trees, creating a trail which sparked and smoldered. I rained down a soft drizzle to quench the earth beneath my feet. A winged demon screeched down from above, claws reaching for my back. Without breaking speed, I dove into a roll and grew a wall of stone from the earth behind me. The creature exploded into a cascade of shimmering elements as it thundered into the barricade. Back on my feet, I slowed to a walk. I came to the edge of a huge ravine, which stood sheer above a raging torrent of black water. On the other side I could see a beautiful garden where golden sunshine shone upon a white figure. It looked like Charlotte. I became desperate to get to the other side. The thought of it really being her overtook my reason.

Frantically, I looked to each side and whipped a thundering wind to tear down the trees around me. Trunks fell and scattered like twigs. I lifted them in pockets of air, stacking them into a narrow log-bridge across the divide between me and the garden. The white figure walked through the field of white flowers, beckoning me to come.

Scrambling across my tree bridge, I inched closer to my goal. I heard a dull rumble, growing louder and louder back inside the jungle. Turning to see the source of the noise I beheld a twisting firestorm shooting through the forest towards the ravine I was perched over. The shining head of Satan roared at the tip of the inferno, mouth open, consuming everything in its path, eating the Elemental jungle, surging ahead to devour me. Panicking, I stumbled, clutching at the trees underneath to keep me from falling into the dark river below. This is a test, I reminded myself. I gathered my wits, heaved myself back up and righted myself on the logs. Closing my eyes and concentrating on the green elements of water in my mind, I pulled a cloud of moisture around me. When I opened my eyes, I was encased in a bubble of water. I looked through and saw Satan's fire spiral towards me. The bubble began to boil and hiss and the fire seared my skin. Orange and red combusted around me. I was burning. With all the focus I could muster, I drew cool water into my body. It soothed me as the roaring cloud of hell passed over. Panting, I let the water rain over me, quenching my steaming body further. Exhausted, I clawed my way over the bridge toward the garden. The white figure in the garden walked towards me. I smiled as it neared, hoping an impossible hope that it was my love. I finally scraped to the other side. The figure looked at me with a thousand eyes and laughed like birds.

"Very good, Michael," the Perceptionist clapped. "Now I will teach you to fly."

SEVEN

ENDLESS DAY, AFTER ENDLESS DAY I honed my power over the elements. My teacher was very pleased with the progress I made. He praised successes and corrected mistakes harshly. I had finally become a master of water, wind, earth and fire. However, I knew nothing of the rest of the elemental spectrum, nothing of spirit and emotion. The Perceptionist flatly refused to show me.

"Do you teach a child calculus before doing basic sums?" he would counter when I asked him. "You cannot handle the power to create life, only to destroy at this point. Only once you've broken things for a thousand years will you truly understand how to fix them. Come to me once you understand this and I'll show you how to create a soul, but no sooner."

My protests fell on deaf ears, but it didn't matter. I was happy with the weapons I had, content they were enough to reap my revenge upon the monster called Gideon. It was time I left my training and tracked him down. I was ready.

I approached The Perceptionist and asked my leave of him. He accepted that I was ready also, and with a nod of his head opened the blue portal that left the void.

"Thank you for your teachings," I said earnestly.

"You were the perfect student," he replied. "I hope you come back to learn the rest one day. There is still much that you're not ready to understand, but I will be here to teach you when you are. Now, return to Hell and seek out an Egyptian named Sokar. He will help you with your resurrection to earth. He will require no payment if you tell him that I sent you. You will need to produce a miniature construction of the sun for him as a sign of my word. Sokar can be found on the west bank of the middle eye of Satan, the lake of sulfur. Good luck and goodbye for now." He disappeared into the void, leaving me alone with no option but to go back through the portal from whence I came.

Marlowe and Phineus looked up from a game of cards they were playing. Germaine was still rocking in the corner, staring at the wall.

"That was quick!" Phineus said. "You mustn't have been longer than five minutes. We've only just dealt our first hand here."

"Oh, he was gone much longer than that, weren't you Michael?" Marlowe interrupted in a knowing tone. "I would say around three months void time?"

"Something closer to a year," I replied. Phineus' eyes bulged and his jaw dropped.

"You mean to tell me time moves differently in the void?" he asked Marlowe.

"Not quite," he replied. "Time doesn't exist in there at all. It is a true void. The Perceptionist created it so he could learn at an accelerated rate while the universe didn't move outside. It's only him and the elements in there, not even space, and without space there is no time."

"I thought I talked in riddles," Phineus laughed. "What do you mean time can't exist without space?"

"Well, time is simply a measure of the amount of space between two points," Marlowe explained. "The 'space' that is between one point in history and another is measured by grades of time such as minutes, hours and days. Just like an inch is the measure of distance between two points in space, time is the measure of distance between two points as well. It is simply using a different dimension."

Phineus looked at Marlowe blankly and then burst out laughing.

"I'll never understand what you're talking about if you try to explain it for a hundred years!" he giggled. "That's fine with me, though, ignorance is bliss sometimes. I'm happy to not know."

"You're either very wise, or very stupid," Marlowe responded.

"Maybe a bit of both," Phineus conceded. "Well," he said standing up, "I guess I'd better fulfill my end of the bargain." Before I could say another word to the prophet, he had disappeared through the portal to the void.

Marlowe smiled at me broadly. "Are you equipped to do what you wish to do?" he asked.

"I am," I said. "Would you walk me out, Marlowe?"

He stood and walked with me, back out into alleyway. I was still wrestling with the fact that I was the son of The Devil.

"Did you like your father, Marlowe?" I asked as we got outside.

"I killed my father," he said without expression. "That is one of the reasons I'm in Hell. I'll never be sorry for doing it. Why?"

"Never mind," I sighed. "I just wonder if Sigmund Freud had a point with his Oedipal complex. I guess he did in your case."

"Freud is a coke-head, gambling addict," Marlowe said bluntly. "You can always find him in Smoking Gun on a Friday night. I wouldn't listen to anything he has to say. I may have killed my father, but I never wanted to do anything sexual with my mother."

I shook my head in amazement. I was still getting used to the idea of souls living on forever in this place; it seemed like such a long time.

"Do you need me to take you anywhere?" Marlowe asked.

"No thanks, my friend, you've done more than enough already by not chopping my head off earlier," I winked. He smiled his white grin again.

"I take it the Perceptionist taught you how to fly," he said. "I'll see you around then, good luck." Without waiting for an answer, Marlowe walked back through the yellow door and shut it behind him.

I was alone in the dark alley again. I felt older and wiser for my visit to the Perceptionist, but my desire for revenge was sharper than ever. I pictured my beautiful Charlotte as I gathered the elements of air around me and used them to lift me off the ground. I would soon be re-born to Earth.

EIGHT

I SOARED THROUGH THE AIR, flying fast and high over the city of Hell, my hair whipping in the wind. It was the single greatest physical thrill I'd ever experienced. I flew at just under the speed of sound toward the Three Eyes of Satan, toward Sokar and the site of my imminent resurrection. The buildings and lights of Hell were a blur of color, streaking past beneath me. This was what it felt like to be a bird.

I slowed my flight as I drew closer to my destination, careful not to fly directly over the flaming lakes; the heat would have been unbearable, even with my cocoon of air around me. I flew down low over the west bank of the middle eye, searching for a sign of the Egyptian, Sokar. The place was deserted, but I spotted a small valley. It split the bank down the middle, nestled in between the lake of fire and the lake of sulfur. I flew lower to get a better look and spied a mud hut nestled next to a large rock outcrop, right in the centre of the valley. I floated around the valley walls, looking for danger. I was full of confidence in my powers, but had learnt never to underestimate any situation during my days as a fighter. I saw no movement and so dropped lightly to the earth, a small distance from the mud hut. It was surprisingly cool between the two lakes, like an oasis in the desert, lined with lush grass and palms. Even ferns grew in between the shadowy nooks of rock that stuck out of the earth at various points. A small waterfall ran down the sheer limestone south wall of the valley. The trickle ran into a stream and eventually pooled into a murky pond to the back of the hut.

I called out to see if I could find anyone around.

"Hello? Sokar?" I bellowed. "I come with word from the Perceptionist."

At the mention of the Elemental's name, a head popped out from inside the mud structure. He had the dark, golden skin of an Egyptian, flawless and beautiful. Atop his head sat a headdress in the shape of a falcon that shone brightly in the shady valley. He emerged completely from the hut and stood to full height. Without the falcon on his head he would have been close to seven feet tall; with it on he looked absolutely giant. He wore a white, cotton skirt with a strip of brown leather tied around him like a belt. Naked from the waist up, his toned stomach muscles rippled as he walked silently toward me. He stopped a few paces away.

"I am Sokar, do you have his seal?" he asked.

Without hesitation, I gathered the elements of air into a ball of hydrogen above my palm, and ignited it with fire. It blazed brightly between us and lit up every shadow in the valley, a perfect miniature of the sun. He smiled in recognition and knelt down, holding up his arms, bathing in the glow of the orb in my palm. After bowing before me six times, worshipping the sun, Sokar motioned to me that he'd seen enough. I quenched the sun with a flood of water from the sky, and he nodded, obviously impressed with my display of power.

"What of the Perceptionist?" he asked in a deep voice fit for a god.

"He has sent me here to be re-born to Earth," I replied simply, not wanting to waste any time with pleasantries. Sokar arched his eyebrow in surprise.

"I hope you died less than a week ago," he said. "Unless, you want to be re-born into a rotting corpse."

"I died three days and three nights ago," I said. With the time in the void, I'd been in Hell much longer, but I knew that barely any time had passed on Earth.

"Very good," he said. "As long as no one has cremated your body, we should be fine. Follow me inside and we will begin."

Sokar strode back inside his hut without waiting for me. I rushed to catch up and entered his home just behind him. It was very plain inside, although much larger than it looked from the front. The floor sank deep below ground level, and opened into a large single room with high ceilings. The only piece of furniture in the place was a straw pallet in the far corner of the room. In the centre there was a fire-pit, which contained glowing coals. The walls were decorated with hieroglyphics that pictured the soul's journey from life to the afterlife.

I walked around the walls slowly, studying the painted images. The closest wall to me showed a young man lying dead on an altar inside a tomb. Seven jars sat beside him and riches were gathered about his mummified body. In the next pictures, the man stood and carried his jars with him up a staircase to the sun and the clouds. He smiled as he reached the top and walked into the blazing light of the gods. These hieroglyphs actually looked like a blend of every different culture's idea of the afterlife, rather than just Egyptian. The next mural showed a different person's life force exiting the body, making his way to a lake. Once at the lake, he paid a toll to a man in a boat and sailed downward, toward the flaming pits of Hell. There, his jars were cast into the fire and he writhed on the ground before the unmistakable figure of Satan. Finally, I made my way to the far wall where a mural pictured the soul's journey in reverse. Men came back down both of the stairs of Heaven, and up the waterfall of Hell. None were smiling. This was the journey from death back to life. It seemed I was definitely in the right place.

Sokar waited patiently for me to finish examining his artistry, and then led me to the middle of the room. He sat down next to the fire-pit, gathering bowls that were scattered on the ground. He dipped his fingers inside one bowl and scooped out some azure-blue paint, smearing it over his face with care, dotting points under his eyes, his chin and his lips before scrawling a curving line on his forehead.

"Lean forward," he said.

I did as he asked and he dotted my face with the paint also. It was cool against my skin. I felt his fingers tracing the same patterns that he'd just drawn on himself. Once finished, Sokar pulled out a knife that was tucked into his belt and picked up an empty bowl at his side.

"Hold out your arm," he instructed firmly. I hesitantly held out my wrist for him, bracing myself for what I knew was coming next. He took the blade and scraped it roughly over my skin, slicing my veins apart. I cried out in pain and he laughed mockingly at me as he caught my gushing blood in the bowl. The wound closed over quickly as my body healed itself, leaving dried blood caked over my arm and hand. Sokar dipped his fingers in my blood and used it to paint his face and then mine with more dots and lines. He looked ghoulish in the dim light, as the embers of the fire threw shadows around the room. Once he'd finished painting his face, he threw the rest of my blood over the coals. A hiss filled the room and my plasma erupted into a red mist that boiled up from the pit.

"Breathe in the fumes," he instructed. I leant over and the iron smell of blood stung my nose. My head began to spin a little.

"You will now begin your journey back to the world of the living," Sokar said in his deep voice. "Envisage how it felt to be inside your body and what the room looked like around you when you died."

I closed my eyes and brought myself back to the painful scene of my death. Charlotte hung, skewered against the wall covered in her own blood. My broken body lay limp on the polished floorboards of my apartment.

"Picture every detail, but picture yourself without injury," Sokar said, and then began to chant in another language.

I imagined myself on the ground unharmed, while I lay and looked up at my love. I looked around the room, my keys sitting on the dining room table next to a pile of men's health magazines. Across the room, Charlotte's bonsais sat in the corner, perfectly manicured to look like trees blowing in the wind. The image of the room wavered as Sokar's chanting grew faster and more frantic. I held onto each detail of the room with every ounce of my will. I began to feel myself slipping out of consciousness. The river of death that welled around my body when I was dying rushed over my body again, drowning me in its turgid waters. It felt like my soul was dying. Suddenly, Sokar's chanting stopped and everything went black.

NINE

THE SMELL OF FAECES WAFTED INTO MY NOSTRILS. I snapped my eyes open and sat up gasping. I lay covered in the excrement that had left my body after I died. I sat there stinking of my own piss and shit. I looked over and saw Lotte's stiff body pinned to the wall. The realization of what had just happened thundered into me. I had been resurrected. My soul had fused once more with my body. I was reborn, but Charlotte was still dead. Looking at my hands, I clenched my fists, making sure I was intact. My body felt strong, despite what it had been through. My muscles ached a little, but I seemed otherwise in perfect health; it was a miracle.

I slowly got to my feet, my head spinning. I stumbled over to where Lotte's body hung and ripped the spikes out of her shoulders, letting her drop gently down into my arms. I'd begun to cry silently. With tears streaming down my face, I carried my love's body to our room and laid her on the bed. I took off her soiled clothes and threw them in the bath of our ensuite. I turned on the shower and stepped under the scalding water, scrubbing blood and shit from my skin as I tore the clothes from my body. I needed to be clean. Frantically, I scoured my skin raw, using a wire brush that Charlotte kept in the shower to clean dead skin from the bottom of her feet. Once I'd grated the muck from my body, I turned the shower off and dried myself. Drops of blood covered my body where I'd scrubbed too hard. At least the blood was my own. Looking in the mirror, I saw myself for the first time since my death. I did indeed look a lot like the devil. We shared the same pointed chin, high cheek bones and jet-black curly hair. But my eyes were much different. They were human. They were jade-green and still glazed with the tears I'd shed for Lotte. I studied my face. Considering I had made a living from violence, it was amazingly clear of scars.

I turned from the mirror and grabbed a clean towel from the bathroom cupboard. Soaking it in warm water, I took it back to Charlotte's body. I cleaned her of the filth that clung to her, washing all traces of the monsters who had raped her. My tears dripped onto the dead skin of her body as I went about my work. Once I had cleaned her fully, I pulled her favorite dress from the wardrobe and dressed her in it. I arranged her arms so they were clasped, resting over her stomach. I went back to the wardrobe, pulled out my best suit and put it on. Lying down next to her on the bed I hugged Lotte as I cried and cried. We were two pieces of the jigsaw together again, but only in body. Part of me wished I could just stay with her forever like that. I lay there for hours sobbing into the pillows that she had slept on, crying into her hair. Finally, I simply went numb. I'd shed every tear left in my body. I kissed Charlotte's cold lips.

"I love you," I whispered into her ear. "I'm going to get the animals that did this to us; I'm going to take them to Hell with me. You will be at rest soon enough, my darling. Our life together is over, but we'll be together again soon, I promise."

I stood up and shifted my perception to view the elements, focusing on fire. The red lights swirled around me. I gathered them all up, massing an inferno in the room, throwing fire into the curtains and against the walls and floor. I focused back to reality and witnessed what I had done. My apartment burned around me, the fire cleansing it of all the sin that had been committed there. Wrapping myself in cool air, I watched as Lotte's body was engulfed in flames, burning away her earthly remains. I turned and walked from the blazing building without looking back, one thing now on my mind: find Gideon.

TEN

I ROAMED THE STREETS AIMLESSLY for hours on end, not really heading anywhere. I didn't go more than a few blocks away from where my apartment had burnt to the ground. Fire engines and police cars flooded the street. I watched from a safe distance as people swarmed in and out of the charred remains of where I used to live. My life there was now dead, but my memories of Charlotte and my knowledge that she was waiting, suffering in limbo burned deep inside.

I had to somehow find Gideon in whatever hole he was hiding. I had no idea where to start, no clues about where to look. I began by scanning the immediate neighborhood's churches. I walked down Filbert Street to The Saints Peter and Paul Cathedral, then down Stockton Street. I thought maybe a man like him would be at a church, but then surely no respectable house of God would accept an over-zealous fanatic like Gideon. He would have his own private place of worship where his followers, The Brethren, went to him. Where?

I went down towards the Harbor where I used to sit with Lotte, watching the seals bathe in the sunshine. North Beach is the heartbeat of San Francisco; its culture and history always inspired me. The streets were packed with people, going about their daily business. Some people sat eating at cafés, while others browsed through clothing stores, looking for something new to wear on the weekend. It all seemed so pointless now I knew there was more to existence. I wanted to scream at them, tell them the truth, but I knew they'd just think I was another crackpot on the sidewalk.

I walked to Pier 39, racking my brain, trying to figure out how I could track down my prey.

I breathed in deeply. The crisp, spring air sent a familiar sharp sting of cold into my throat. I loved how it felt. The tangy salt air of the real world revitalized me. I concentrated on how it felt to have oxygen enter my lungs and exit noisily through my nose. My stomach moaned painfully as I became aware of my mortal shell. All fluids had exited my body when I died. I was empty. My head started to spin. I needed food.

Ravenous, I ran across the road to the oceanfront, where one of my favorite Italian restaurants sat. I ate a huge plate of vegetarian pasta. It tasted amazing. I hadn't eaten at all in Hell, as there was no need. I hadn't realized how much I missed it. The simple, physical sensations of life on earth stood out now as incredible. The contrast between life and death was startling. A zing of pepper on my tongue tingled every nerve in my body. I had never enjoyed the sensation of eating so much. However, it did nothing to quell my insatiable hunger. I needed meat. I needed blood.

I ordered two large steaks, extra rare. They came out with roasted vegetables, which I swept from the plate. I picked up the pieces of meat with my hands. Gnawing and gulping the flesh, I swallowed it down as fast as I could. I licked the pink blood of the steaks from my fingers after each gluttonous bite. I savored its metallic taste. By the time I'd finished, every diner in the place was staring at me, stunned by my vampire-like behavior. Now full, I became conscious of my actions. I got up and left immediately. I didn't need to be drawing any attention to myself after just burning down my apartment with Lotte's body inside.

With the disturbing appetite satisfied, my mind turned back to the real hunger inside my soul: the hunger for revenge. I searched my mind for answers about where I could find Gideon, but still I was blank. I was getting nowhere. I had to do something. Go back to the beginning, I thought.

I walked back towards my apartment and came upon a newsstand. My mind clicked into gear with a possibility. I bought every newspaper on the shelf and then went out into the street to find a quiet place to read them. Finding a good spot, I scanned all of the papers for any mention of a new cult, brain-washing followers gullible enough to join. There was nothing. I read every paper I could get my hands on from front to back. Each one was the same; the world was fucked -- terrorism, climate change, swine flu, but no mention of Gideon or his brethren. By now it was almost dawn. I sat leafing through old papers on a bench at the front of an abandoned church. Its doors were boarded up with a large yellow and black sign out the front that said: 'Condemned Building UNSAFE'. I sat there hoping Gideon would just walk past. Then it struck me. I didn't need to find him. I would make him find me.

As soon as they were open, I went to the headquarters of every newspaper in town and took out the same full-page ad in every one. It read:

> *To Gideon and The Brethren.*
> *Michael is alive. God will be angry.*
> *You can find him at the church closest to where he last lay.*

Only Gideon, or someone present at my murder, would have any idea what the ad meant, or which church I was talking about. There were hundreds of churches in San Francisco, if not thousands, and the fact that this church was condemned meant the only people coming inside would be my enemies.

I had one day at least to prepare myself, since the ad wouldn't run until the next morning. I went out and bought some netting and steel wire, some lead weights, video cable, a camera and a small television. Once I had my supplies, I stashed them in the church grounds and waited for night to fall. As soon as the sun set, I went to work. I cut a peephole at the door of the church and rigged the video camera to the T.V. I placed it up in the ceiling where I could sit in the rafters, watching and waiting for Gideon and his followers to arrive. I then rigged up a snare with my netting and weights, ready to entangle anyone who walked through the front doors of the church. I wanted to use an earthly trap before I fell back on my elemental powers. No point in giving away the advantage of surprise unnecessarily.

There was one other entrance to the church, which was through the Vicar's demolished living quarters. I made sure this way was well and truly blocked, so the only way in was through the front doors. The scene of Gideon and our final showdown was set. Forming a cushion of air from the elements for myself, I perched up in the darkest corner of the high church ceiling in front of my crude surveillance system and waited.

I sat and fumed, imagining the revenge I was to reap on Gideon and anyone stupid enough to follow him into the church. My chest constricted and my stomach twisted with the nervous night of waiting. It was like someone was using my insides as a stress ball. During the whole night, every peep and creak in the church jerked me to attention, but I grew dead tired, not having rested since I had been reborn nearly forty-eight hours before. I slowly began to fall into a fitful, troubled sleep. I dreamt that Gideon entered the church with an army of followers who tore the house of God apart before consigning it to flames. I burned alive still sleeping on my rafters, not waking because I'd become so used to the stifling heat in Hell. My skin melted and dripped from my bones to the floor where it eventually evaporated. I had no body left. I then lay screaming in Hell, not in pain but in devastation that I had no vessel to be resurrected into. I could never be reborn to even the score with Gideon.

I jolted awake. It was midday at least. Sunshine poured through the windows, casting dusty-grey beams of light around the congregation floor. I looked down below me and surveyed the church in the light. There were cracked and broken floorboards everywhere, some had been pulled up and scattered to every corner of the church. A vandal had broken

181

all the pews inside and piled them like a large pyre underneath where Jesus still hung crucified on his cross, a bloody crown of thorns perched on his head. There was a large, upside-down pentacle, the star of Satan, spray-painted in red over his chest, presumably by the same person that had broken the furniture. It had always struck me as odd how Christians worshipped this image of Jesus, yet the second of the Ten Commandments was not to create images of God's likeness. Moses had decreed in the name of God that, "You shall not make yourself an image, whether in the form of anything that is in Heaven above, or that is on the earth beneath, or that is in the water underneath the earth." According to the Holy Trinity, Jesus was God, as was the Father, the Son and the Holy Spirit -- not just His Son. So why were they allowed to reproduce his likeness, to worship en masse? It was one of the many contradictions that puzzled me about the modern church.

I looked at Jesus hanging there with the star of Satan on his chest and thought of Gideon. How could Jesus' supposed message of love and forgiveness get so twisted by the human mind? It was time I made Gideon pay for his sins. There would be no forgiveness for him in the hell I was sending him to. It was time for my revenge.

The shadows in the room grew longer and darker as the day progressed, with no sign of Gideon or his followers. My eyes began to ache from watching the T.V. screen which sat inches from my face. People walked by on the street, paying no attention to the church, no idea what lay inside. I decided that Gideon would not dare enter the church in broad daylight. He would wait until nightfall, if he were to come at all. I grew frustrated, itching for him to come. I needed him to come. Soon the sun set, but still no sign of my prey. Maybe he didn't see the ad; maybe he was too scared to enter the church. Maybe he knew what I was up to.

"Don't be stupid," I said, talking to myself, going delirious. "Of course he doesn't know your plan, how can he? He might be suspicious, but curiosity will get the better of him."

I settled myself by imagining all the terrible things I was going to do to him. I grew patient and silent once more, and the evening wore on. Just when I had given up hope of anyone coming that night, I saw a flicker of movement on the monitor. I looked intently and saw the dark shape of a single, hooded figure approaching the door at a slow, creeping walk. Gideon!

ELEVEN

THE FIGURE OF GIDEON STOPPED and looked behind him out to the street, checking that no one was following him. His face was shrouded in a white hood. He walked past the camera without looking up and cracked open the front door, peering inside tentatively. I waited patiently. I had waited this long, what was a few more minutes? I needed him to walk all the way inside for me to spring my trap. He inched inside and crept through the church, looking from side to side, waiting for an attack. When it didn't come he walked slowly across the room, searching the pitch-black shadows inside, probably for my unconscious body. After what seemed like an eternity, he stood right in the centre of my web.

I sprang my trap into action, tumbling the heavy lead-weights to the floor. The wire cable tied to the weights pulled tight, and the net wrapped up and tangled around him. He struggled and flailed in my snare as I laughed in victory. His high-pitched, girl-like screams rang around the church. He hung trapped in my netting, high off the ground, wailing like a caged animal. I cut the cable and let him fall, crashing to the ground. Leaping from my hiding place, I floated on air softly to the ground. I rushed to where he lay groaning and ripped the hood back from his face, to reveal a semi-conscious teenage girl.

"What?" I roared in frustration. The girl had dirt all over her face and was dressed in ragged clothes, a homeless urchin child. She moaned as her eyes slid open at my primal growls of rage. She looked up at me, questioningly.

"The man outside said he'd pay me ten dollars if I found his necklace in here," she groaned. "Do you have it? What happened? I think my legs are broken." My heart sunk to my boots; it was a trap!

I raised my head towards the front door and a pair of dark legs blocked my vision. I looked up to see Gideon swinging a blazing white sword of fire toward my face.

I dove to the side as Gideon's scorching blade sizzled past my head. I rolled away as he approached me. The homeless girl screamed behind him in terror. He turned and silenced her with a well-aimed kick to the temple. She fell to the ground either dead or unconscious, I wasn't sure which. By now I was on my feet and ready.

"So," Gideon hissed through clenched teeth. "You've come back to kill me? You fool! If you do, I'll just go to Heaven into the arms of God."

"You'll come to Hell with me, you devil," I shouted and hurled a ball of air into his stomach, knocking him clean off his feet and crashing through some of the broken floorboards behind him. The flame of his sword died as he dropped it, clattering to the floor. I walked slowly toward him as he lay crumpled on the ground. I savored the moment. My first victory was close at hand.

"You were stupid to come alone," I snarled at him. "You underestimate my powers, you vile creature. I have the power of Satan in me."

I gathered a large fireball between my hands, ready to send his stinking soul down to Hell where I could torture him, wringing God's secret from him between screams.

I raised the fire above my head and screamed, "For Charlotte!" as I prepared to hurl it at Gideon. I was at full stretch when I was struck heavily from behind. I hit the ground with a thud, quenching the ball of flame before it could burn up into my body. Doubled over in pain, I could feel blood seeping out of a wound in the back of my head, gushing over my shoulders and neck. I rolled onto my back and looked up through starry vision, to see a large, bearded man dressed in white. He was holding a baseball bat caked in blood and hair. He smiled as he looked down at me. I could see he was missing most of his teeth.

"I got him, Gideon," he said in a simpleton's voice. "I smashed him good."

I lay still on the ground gathering my wits. The sound of shuffling feet indicated more people entering the church. It appeared Gideon wasn't silly enough to come alone after all. He had brought his Brethren.

Reaching slowly behind my head I felt my skull. The skin was split badly, but the bone was intact. I wasn't seriously injured from the blow, but was losing lots of blood. I would need to close the wound. Pulling elements of fire to my fingers I cauterized the gash, stemming the flow of blood. I let out a grunt of pain as the flesh sizzled together.

Feigning serious injury I looked around the room, assessing the situation. I counted how many enemies had come to die. There were twelve gathered around me in a half circle, all staring down waiting for orders from their master. Most were men, but there were two women as well. All were dressed in white. The one that had hit me stood in the middle, holding his bat ready in case I moved. If I'd wanted to, I could have killed him where he stood, but I chose to wait. Gideon walked into the circle and stood over me, a line of blood seeping from the corner of his mouth. It felt good to know I'd hurt him.

"Here we are again," he said. "You lying helpless on the ground and me in control. Your parlor tricks are no match for the power of God."

My hatred seethed inside as I watched him; I would soon wipe that smug smile from his face.

"Pick him up," Gideon ordered. Three of his stinking followers leant in to grab me. Without moving off the ground, I whipped up the elements of air underneath their feet and lifted them off the ground, flipping them upside down and raising them slowly in the air. The others gasped in shock and retreated backward, but Gideon held firm, not taking his eyes off me. I could hear the three wailing in fear as I sent them higher in the air until they were pinned against the ceiling. I held them, looking into Gideon's eyes, and then let them drop. Their screams, which filled the church as they fell, cut short as soon as they crashed down onto the floor, splintering the boards beneath them, dead. The others in the room cried out, but Gideon held up his arms to silence them.

"Do not fear this demon," he said soothingly. "If your body dies today you will go to Heaven as I have promised."

"Give me God's secret and I will show mercy on your flock of sheep, Gideon." I replied flatly. "If you don't, I will crush them before your eyes."

"You are the one who shall be crushed," he snarled. "I will send you back down to Hell where you belong. Now finish him!" he shouted and waved his arm forward. The Brethren advanced. I laughed at how helpless they were, it was somewhat pathetic. I felt a fleeting moment of pity for them. The feeling passed quickly.

Shifting my perception to view the elements at hand, I set to destroy them all, one by one. I built a wall of air around myself so none of them could get close enough to touch me. Then began the bloodbath.

The man with the bat came first. I rained boulders from nothingness onto his thick head, crushing him beneath their weight so he lay pinned, bleeding to death on the ground. Three more climbed over him and I froze them in their tracks, holding them with air. I then gathered the element of water above them and poured a deluge down their throats, drowning them. Their stomachs bloated and expanded under the pressure of the flood entering their bodies. Suddenly, all three burst apart like over-filled water balloons, showering blood and skin all over the church. I laughed in victory, looking at Gideon. He didn't move, he just watched as I continued to annihilate his followers.

One of the women screamed as she ran at me from the left. I threw a jet of fire into her and she crackled into flames, screeching as she burned alive. Finally, she fell to her knees silently and dropped dead on her face. I quenched the fire around her so the church would not catch ablaze. Another came forward and I forced helium elements inside his body through the pores of his skin. I expanded the helium, and then set it alight. He evaporated in a hiss of steam. The last three I rounded up with a barrier of air as they sobbed and begged for mercy. I looked each of them in the eyes and saw pure fear. I felt sorry for them. They had been led astray by Gideon and had received nothing but empty promises.

"Leave here," I said to them. "You are not the ones I want. Gideon has sinned. He is no messenger of God. He has sent both you and this poor homeless girl into certain destruction. He has raped and killed an innocent woman, my beautiful wife. Is that the will of a loving Lord? Go back to your families and forget what happened here. Don't say a word of what you have seen to anyone, or I will come back and bring you down to Hell myself." I released their bonds and they ran crying, out of the doors and into the empty street. Gideon and I were alone.

TWELVE

"IT'S YOUR TURN TO DIE NOW," I sneered at Gideon. He stood unmoving, exactly where he had been during the entire massacre of his followers.

"You don't even care for them," I taunted. "You let them die for no reason."

He broke into his smug grin once more and laughed.

"Yes, I did let them die," he said. "But they did not die in vain, they showed me something very valuable. That your powers are weak, while mine are strong."

With inhuman speed he ran at me, catching me off guard. Surging forward he rammed into me at full charge, knocking me backwards onto floor. I crashed down flat on my back, oxygen wheezing out of my lungs. I stumbled to my feet, winded, looking around for him. He was now at the end of the church, arms stretched toward the sky, chanting. I felt the air thicken around my body and tighten. I couldn't move!

I struggled to free myself, my mind in shock. How did he do that? How could he command the elements like me? I changed my perception to view the elements that held me, looking to see if I could unwrap my bonds. To my horror, I saw that they were not elements of air but of spirit, the elements that I had no power to control! I was helpless. I panicked and convulsed, trying to get free. Gideon's condescending laugh echoed through the church as he walked towards me. I looked back to him as he cackled, feeling like a helpless infant in his grasp. Even more, I felt the sharp spite that I held for him, the one who killed my Charlotte.

"You think God would not arm me against the likes of you?" he sneered as he circled around me. "He has made me a brother to dragons, and a companion to owls. I have watched you wield your pitiful powers against the Brethren and have seen your weakness. You only use the four basest of elements. You have no control over spirit, no control over the mind. You will never beat me, or God. You cannot defeat the boundless power of the one true Elemental! "

"His power is not endless nor is He the only elemental," I snapped, trying to throw him off balance. "You know his flaws intimately, you know He isn't all powerful or all knowing, you who holds his secret."

He laughed again. "Is that what you think His secret is? Is that what you think I know?" he asked. "I know what you think," he continued in his boyish voice. "You think that God has created a prison for himself, one He could not escape from if he was to be locked inside."

"That is what I know already," I said baiting him.

"You're right, Michael, he did make the prison." Gideon smirked. "He made it just after the creation of man and trapped himself inside not long after."

"So he is helpless," I taunted. "He is trapped in a cage of his making, unable to get out."

Gideon threw his head back and roared with mocking laughter.

"You mean he *was* trapped, Michael. If he was still inside how could He have given me these glorious powers?" Gideon tightened the bonds holding me until I felt I was going to burst.

"He has only in the last century figured out how to escape. In fact, He has only figured out in the last century that He actually was trapped."

I was suddenly puzzled. What was this monster talking about?

"You speak lies," I said coolly. "You know nothing of God's true secret."

"It is you who knows nothing. You who has been lied to," he snapped back. "God has told me all. He even told me the name of His prison. He called it Hell, the stifling world that you have lived in until recently."

My heart leapt to my throat. This could not be!

"He told me how He trapped himself down there and locked Himself out at the same time," Gideon continued. "God imprisoned half of His mind inside a second body, so He couldn't figure a way out. He locked out His own knowledge of what he'd done. He didn't even really know who He was, did not even *try* to escape." Gideon walked back to the front of me and shoved his face right up to mine, spraying spittle over me as he talked. "God even gave Himself a purpose down there, a purpose that would help keep him from seeking out the truth, a task that needed to be carried out anyway."

What was this demon talking about? I didn't know. He continued to talk.

"After the longest time God realized He was not complete, that there was another side to His being. That the adversary He hated most was in fact himself."

I was lost in Gideon's words. I looked to the image of Jesus nailed to the crucifix on the wall behind him, the sign of the devil on his chest glowing red. The meaning of Gideon's ranting speared through my head like a spike of hot metal. He was saying that God *was* the Devil, that they were the same being!

I convulsed again, struggling to get free, roaring in anger at the lies Gideon was trying to inject like poison into my brain. He pressed on as I tore against my bonds with my mind.

"God realized that he was Satan and now wants to be whole again. He wants to be the truly complete being he was when he created the universe. However, he needs someone to rehabilitate the souls in Hell so they can still go to Heaven. He dare not leave that place unguarded, lest the Perceptionist and the other demons corrupt every soul entering beyond redemption. God needed a son to take his place, he needed you, Michael, and so He created you; someone who would live the sins of earth and therefore

191

know how to purge them. Someone with His power, but with a human soul, one that would never be clean enough to ever enter Heaven. But that bitch came along and started to mess with His plans, so He sent me to kill her."

At the mention of Charlotte, a furious rage boiled up inside me the likes of which I had never felt. It destroyed my reason. It became my justification. Red seeped over my vision and then turned to something else. My perspective changed to an angle I had never seen before. I saw clearly the swirling of Gideon's soul in front of me. The gold, silver and green of his person twisted in a bubbling mass before me, contained within his body. I saw it and I loathed it. I wanted to destroy it. I needed to. Pure hatred drove me as I saw the weakness in its construction. There were tiny breaks between the elements of his essence, where they were fused together. With a defiant growl I threw my anger inside him, forcing black elements of hate between the gaps of his soul. Gideon moved to resist me, throwing a barrage of wind and fire into my body. I didn't relent. I tore him apart, not just his body but his true being. I ripped up each element that contained his life-force and dispelled them into the air. I ravaged his heart and flayed his spirit. I murdered his soul. I shattered it. I sent Gideon screaming into oblivion for all the pain he had caused me and Charlotte.

THIRTEEN

I COLLAPSED TO THE GROUND panting, spewing the contents of my insides, retching vomit onto the floor as I fell to my knees. I'd just committed murder. Not just murder of the body, but the first ever murder of the soul.

There was nothing more for Gideon. He was nowhere. I had utterly destroyed him. He was gone. His soul was now just scattered elements in the air, with no consciousness, no spirit, nothing. A great sadness overcame me. There was no chance of redemption for me now and I knew it. I had just committed the ultimate sin in the eyes of God. I had splintered one of his creations into a million pieces, never to be resurrected, never to feel pain or joy or sorrow again. The finality of it stunned me.

I knelt there sobbing; spit dripping from my mouth like a baby as I wept on all fours. Grief consumed me: grief for Charlotte, grief for Gideon and grief for myself. I'd become a monster in my quest for revenge, a monster created through circumstance. I was blind to my inevitable fate. If only I hadn't talked to Charlotte on that plane, would this have turned out differently? How could I have stopped this if fate was against me? At least she would have been spared.

Soon my grief turned back to rage. Was this supposed to be the fate that God and The Devil had created for me by manipulating my path? How dare they use me as their puppet and decide my soul's final destination. Is this what they wanted of me? I refused to believe that this was the end of it.

Another more glaring question hung in my mind. Was Gideon telling me the truth about God, or were they just more of his lies? There was only one way to find out for sure. I pulled myself to my feet. I wobbled as I stumbled past the limp bodies of the Brethren, scattered over the floor of the church. I checked the young homeless girl; she was dead as well, another innocent victim of religion. I walked to the back wall where Jesus hung, the stack of broken wood piled beneath him. Gathering the elements of fire around me, I ignited the pyre, along with the rest of the church.

Flames licked the effigy of Jesus. As his body began to burn, so did mine. The searing heat of fire reaped our bodies as one. I threw myself onto the burning coals beneath Jesus and waited for death to swamp around me. Pain filled every fiber of my body, as my insides bubbled and blistered. I didn't care. I wanted to be back in Hell. I would find the answers I was looking for, even if I had to tear them from Satan's throat.

The church began to collapse in on itself, just as I felt blissful death wash over my body. My bones were charred and my body gone, but my purpose still raged inside like the fire that destroyed everything around me.

I'm not finished, I thought, as I died for the second time.

FOURTEEN

I KNEW THE MAN SITTING IN FRONT OF ME. He preferred to be called Asmodeus, but his name was Satan. He was my unwanted father, and right now I hated the sight of him.

I stood bound by immoveable elements wrapped so tight around me that I couldn't even blink. I was held firm as his eyes bored inside me. I knew by the way he looked at me that Gideon had been telling the truth. This was not only Satan, it was also God. His eyes revealed his true self to me. It was inside him; inside his shadow that hung menacing on the wall, flickering in the firelight. He sat patiently watching me, deciding the best way to explain to me why he had carried out the despicable things he'd done to Charlotte. I didn't need him to tell me. I had already guessed. He told me anyway.

He stood up and leaned on his chair.

"Michael, when I told you that the first being that I made was Satan, I wasn't lying. I created him of my own consciousness. I did not know how to create a being from scratch just yet, so I divided myself in two, like a split personality in two bodies. I poured all my hate, envy, fear and contempt into this new side of me, and kept compassion, empathy and love in the other. I named the being Lucifer. At first it was like there was a one-way mirror between us. I could see and feel and know both sides, but Lucifer could only see himself and it interested me how he acted."

He paused and waited for me to react, but I did not. He started to pace around the room in front of me, becoming more animated as he spoke.

"The connection between Lucifer and me soon began to grow cloudier, as I started to despise the things this side of me did." he continued. "Lucifer started to act independently from my conscious will. Slowly, we became truly separate beings, and he began calling himself Satan. As this Satan, he had the capacity for cruelty. He would attack the imperfections in my creations, as I engineered the universe. He ridiculed me for what he called my 'grotesque children': humans. But aside from this cruelty, he also had the capacity for great intellect and foresight. He invented the absolute necessity of death on earth, so life evolved and changed rather than sailing around in circles. Through his intellect he also developed a twisted system of morality. He believed it was only right that humans be treated equally, no matter what. He believed that they should all come to Heaven after death and enjoy a blissful, pain-free existence. He argued that because they were imperfect they shouldn't have to be punished. I could not allow that. People have to be made responsible for their actions, even if they made their choices while ignorant of all the facts. However, I didn't have the stomach to punish them for their wrong-doings. I needed Satan to do it for me. Only he had the ability to do the essential things I could not bring myself to do, the things I could not cope with doing. In my last moment of clarity, I created a prison for this side of me. It is the place you know as Hell. It was not just made to contain this side of myself, but also as a penitentiary for the corrupted souls of earth. Satan could punish and rehabilitate these souls without mercy, cleansing them so they could eventually pass over and enjoy the fruits of Heaven with me. I cast him down to this prison and we were blocked off totally. I shut out all memory of how he'd been originally created. I only knew of what he did if I heard indirectly from the angels or humans, and he knew nothing of me."

The Devil was wringing his hands and staring into space as he recounted his story. It was as if he was telling the tale to himself, rather than to me.

"The angels didn't know the truth of Satan's origins, and I never knew to tell them. We went on thinking we were separate beings for thousands of years. We grew to hate each other. I deplored him for the things he did to my souls as he carried out his brutal work. He cleansed their souls with fire, so that Hell wouldn't fill up and overflow with despicable beings. Satan's hate for me seethed over the centuries. It bubbled and festered like a wound that doesn't heal. Eventually, he began on his quest for Armageddon. He wanted to destroy me and I was happy to destroy him, as I didn't fully realize the necessity of his work. My hate had blinded me into thinking these souls could be cleansed through the power of love alone. Satan soon figured out how to escape Hell, onto Earth.

"I went down from Heaven to stop him from defiling my wonderful masterpiece creation. We finally met on Earth, and came face to face for the first time since I had cast him into Damnation. At once, we both realized the horrible truth: that we'd been fighting ourselves the whole time. I also immediately realized that as a split being I had relinquished the full capacity to enjoy life and the full capacity of omnipotence. I was a shell, and I wanted my entire-self back. We made peace and planned to make ourselves whole once more. It took a while to figure out how to fuse our souls back together as one. After many failed attempts, I finally succeeded. I destroyed my old body and poured my godly soul into the more resilient form that I had created in Satan. I was now God Asmodeus. I was now ready to return to Heaven, but there was still one major problem. This is where you came in, Michael."

He looked at me with his dark eyes. I sat silently and listened. I didn't even think anything, lest my thoughts give me away. Beads of sweat poured down my forehead in the effort it took to control my rage. As I watched Asmodeus before me, I could see two distinct sides of him. While he talked, his countenance changed from a smile to a frown every few seconds. His eyes twitched, he blinked erratically and stared off into space, mid-sentence. It was like his two personalities were not properly joined as a single soul. They were wrestling for dominance inside his body. I got the impression that the evil side was winning.

God brought himself under control; sighing, he continued his story.

"I wanted to be whole and live up in my sanctuary of Heaven," he said "but I could not leave my beautiful corrupted souls to rot inside Hell for all eternity, I could not bear it. I needed a caretaker. Someone would have to rule Hell for me, a person who could carry out the necessary evils that my former self hadn't been able to commit to. I considered asking the Perceptionist, but he is too unpredictable. I needed someone who I could trust, so I birthed a son. That son is you, Michael."

God waited for his news to affect me. When it did not, he looked confused at my patience but pressed on regardless.

"I needed a soul guaranteed to come to Hell once its body had died on earth. So, as Satan, I planted my seed into a whore. She did as I wanted, and gave you up into a life of despair. This was meant to corrupt the human side of your spirit just as many of the corrupted souls of earth. You were supposed to become one of few creations that would become so distorted and steeped in sin that you would be without redemption. You could rule with an iron fist for eternity and ensure Hell was the place it needed to be."

God's face constricted again into a snarl and he turned his back on me, pacing back and forth, mumbling to himself. He quickly brought himself under control and turned to face me again.

"My plans were spoiled by an innocent, Charlotte," he said, smiling falsely. "She came to you by total luck, through free will. It all happened by coincidence, she changed her plane ticket to come home early from a holiday and ended up sitting next to you. She began to ruin my plans and rehabilitated your soul with the power of her love. It was an unacceptable disaster. You would be lost to Heaven while I was stuck managing the souls in Hell, not the other way around."

This was definitely Satan talking.

"Luckily, I saw the opportunity in this mistake. I was blind to think that you could manage Hell properly without the capacity to love, so I let your relationship blossom, let it grow to the purest of loves. Then I took it from you."

I stared blankly at him, hating him with every element inside my soul, but I hid my hate and sat still. He pleaded with me to understand, almost groveling as he went on.

"I had to take her, Michael. By trapping Charlotte in limbo, creating a lost soul that was attached to yours, I was ensuring that you would never, ever be able to forgive me. You will never be able to rest until she rests, and I will *never* let her into Heaven. You will forever be trapped in Hell where you can rule, where you *must* rule. I can see it inside you now; even as you hate me, you still love her. It is the perfect combination to be able to administer my souls: the human condition to love and hate at the same time."

Finally, I broke my silence.

"Why didn't you just tell me all of this the first time I came screaming into Hell? Why would you put me through further pain and suffering to come to the same end?"

He actually cracked into a smile, and licked his lips with his forked tongue.

"To give you the *power* to rule," he explained. "You were weak when you first came to me. I could not have someone so weak reign over my souls. They would have ripped you apart. You had the divine power inside you, but you had to take this path to learn the power of the elements. So, I sent you on the track to meet the Perceptionist. He was the only other one who could teach you what you needed to know, while I made preparations for my final departure. You learnt the power from him and had the desire to carry out what needed to be done. However, I wanted proof that you would exercise your abilities if needed.

"I set up your second meeting with Gideon to take you to the next level. It was easy to trick him into facing you, he trusted me completely. With the power to control the soul, and the power to destroy it, you went back to Earth to your destiny. I hoped your hate would be so pure that you could bring yourself to tear a soul to pieces. I could never bring myself to do it, not even as Satan. It was the one necessity I could not carry out. There are souls down here that will never be able to enter Heaven. They will never be redeemed. These are the souls you must destroy, for they have become worthless. You will be able to take out the trash that isn't wanted anymore." He licked his lips again and continued.

"This path was also designed to show you the many souls that can still be saved from Hell; it taught you to love them. Souls like Smithy and Mack. They are down here because they refuse to forgive themselves for their crimes; they need to understand I forgive them because they are just human. All they need to do is accept my redemption and they will come to Heaven and into my open arms of love. "

"There will be no forgiveness for you," I spat. "There will be no redemption for the things you have done to me and to all of the souls down here!" I felt a surge of power from my anger and burst from his bonds that held me. I stood up enraged.

"You shall not have what you desire. Do you think I will do your bidding after what you have done to us? Do you think I will let you just go back to Heaven and sit on your throne to lap up the love of the souls I send cleansed up to you? Never!" I threw a chair that stood next to me against the wall in my fury as I screamed at God.

"I will corrupt them further. I will turn them against you and make them see why they should hate you. You may have created us, but you do not rule us, we rule ourselves. I am not afraid of you. I will destroy you!" I shouted and surged forward with a swarm of hatred around me, intending to kill Him, intending to snuff out His life force as I had snuffed out Gideon's. I could not. He began to laugh as I threw a barrage of rage through His soul. It simply washed through Him, like water straining through a sieve. I pummeled my anger and hate into Him but it was useless.

"You cannot destroy the creator," He bellowed. "I do not seek forgiveness from you. In fact, I count on your eternal hatred, but you will do as I say. I am the one true Elemental God who made you what you are! I know your weaknesses and

I know your desires, I know all!" He shouted as He flung me sprawling across the room and held me tight again.

"I am going to my kingdom of Heaven now and I am going to leave you to yours. Do what your freewill wants you to do, I am sure it will lead you down the right path," He said and turned his back on me, evaporating into His own shadow. I threw the fire of wrath after Him, but He was gone.

I stormed around the room in a rage, a maelstrom of hate and disgust. I battered at the walls of the room around me and punched the floors, sapping myself of all energy. Finally, I collapsed in a heap on the ground.

I was defeated.

FIFTEEN

I HAVE NOT MOVED NOW FOR A YEAR. I have sat here on the floor of this doleful room and thought of all that transpired over the course of my being. I have come, in time, to realize this: I could have done nothing to change my destiny up to this point, but I control everything I do from here on in.

I sit here in Hell and I am resolute, my body electric with motivation. I will build an army from God's corrupted souls and turn them further against Him. I will recruit them to my cause, which will be the ultimate destruction of God.

The Perceptionist told me once that there was no such thing as an all powerful, all knowing being. It is an impossibility. I will seek out God's weakness if it takes me all of eternity. I will destroy Him. I will have my revenge.

The true battle between God and Satan begins now, but I am the Satan, I am the adversary.

God is not pure. He is not righteous. He is flawed. The God Elemental thinks He is benevolent, that He can do no wrong simply because He has no one to answer to. Well, I will become the one who will judge God for *His* sins. I will make Him pay and then I will recover my love, Charlotte, from her prison in limbo.

I do not pretend to be all-knowing, or all-powerful. I am human, but I will prevail. I will destroy this brat deity and create the new world how it should be, with no suffering and no sorrow.

I will expose God for what He really is: a malevolent charlatan of the highest degree. I will conquer the universe through the power of truth, and I will do it with the help of all the lost souls in Hell.

When the time comes, will you join me?